MW00932806

THE
GRAY

THE GRAY

CHRIS BARON

FEIWEL AND FRIENDS
NEW YORK

A FEIWEL AND FRIENDS BOOK

An imprint of Macmillan Publishing Group, LLC

120 Broadway, New York, NY 10271

mackids.com

Copyright © 2023 by Chris Baron. All rights reserved.

Our books may be purchased in bulk for promotional,
educational, or business use. Please contact your local bookseller
or the Macmillan Corporate and Premium Sales Department
at (800) 221-7945 ext. 5442 or by email at
MacmillanSpecialMarkets@macmillan.com.

Library of Congress Cataloging-in-Publication Data

Names: Baron, Chris (Christopher Leigh), author.
Title: The Gray / Chris Baron.
Description: First edition. | New York : Feiwel and Friends, 2023. |
    Audience: Ages 10–14 | Audience: Grades 7–9 | Summary: Sasha
    has been bullied at his middle school and his anxiety, which he
    calls the Gray, is growing, so his parents and therapist suggest a
    summer in the country with his aunt might help him.
Identifiers: LCCN 2022046356 | ISBN 9781250864710 (hardcover)
Subjects: CYAC: Anxiety—Fiction. | LCGFT: Novels.
Classification: LCC PZ7.1.B3717 Gr 2023 | DDC [Fic]—
    dc23/eng/20230206
LC record available at https://lccn.loc.gov/2022046356

First edition, 2023
Book design by Trisha Previte
Printed in the United States of America by Lakeside Book Company,
Harrisonburg, Virginia
Feiwel and Friends logo designed by Filomena Tuosto

ISBN 978-1-250-86471-0 (hardcover)

1 3 5 7 9 10 8 6 4 2

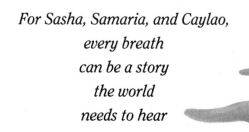

For Sasha, Samaria, and Caylao,
every breath
can be a story
the world
needs to hear

PROLOGUE

All my plans for the summer are ruined.

I unplug my Alien 5000 laptop that took forever for me to configure just right, wrap the cord around it, and hand it to my dad. "Be careful with this, please," I say.

"It's going to be worth it, Sasha," he says. "We discussed this. Change is good. Be tough."

This, as I give him all my devices: my smartwatch, my tablet, even my new Nintendo Switch. He lets me keep my phone, but only so I can stay in touch.

This will be the worst summer ever.

My friend Daniel and I were going to have marathon gaming sessions playing Earthforge, watch YouTube all night, and do lots of sleepovers. Daniel even got a new VR headset we were supposed to try out together.

I send what might be my last text to Daniel. *See you when we start eighth grade!* I glance at my reflection in the phone—the only thing this screen will be useful for soon.

I can't believe I have to spend a device-free summer upstate with my aunt Ruthie, who doesn't have Wi-Fi or even a computer.

Worst. Summer. Ever.

I hug Dad goodbye. He hugs me back with arms made of iron. Like he could still lift me up and throw me around.

"I love ya," he says, holding up his fist. "Stay grounded." I bump his fist with mine and lean in a little more before letting go. He likes saying this, but staying grounded has always been hard for me. My heart thumps against my chest. I try breathing through it.

When Doctor Winters told my parents that one of the reasons I need a break is because I am "overwhelmed by technology," I didn't want to believe him. Grown-ups are always telling us that video games and devices hurt us. But that isn't completely true. Phones, laptops, tablets, gaming—these things are just part of who we are. My parents don't get it. When I told Dr. W this, he actually agreed with me. He said that technology is important, that it is a part of our lives, that it even saves lives. But he also said that everyone's situation is different—that my situation is different.

Dr. W said a lot of complicated things. At first, he thought I had something called heightened sensitivity with social anxiety, or another thing he called a panic disorder, but after a while he said that maybe when my senses get overwhelmed, what I seem to be experiencing is what he calls generalized anxiety with occasional panic.

It still sounds complicated. When something gets a name, it can become an even bigger thing—and it's easier for people to use it against you.

Lots of people get anxious, but not everyone gets anxious like I do sometimes. I see or feel too much or have super-realistic dreams. Tight spaces can feel like being held down; loud noises are a megaphone in my ear. Crowded places just make me want to hide. Dr. W has his own labels for it. He says it's an "exacerbation that comes from an overuse and overdependence on technology."

I heard my parents talking about it after I was supposed to be asleep. My dad didn't want to tell the school. He wants us to get through it on our own. But my mom said it was the right thing to do, so she talked to the principal. No one asked if *I* want anyone to know about it, which I *don't*. Everyone already thinks I'm different—too sensitive, a little weird.

And ever since my uncle Lou died, everything has gotten worse. When I get overwhelmed, it feels like I go to a different place—it's like I'm in a different world. I call it the Gray.

1

"So, Sasha-bug. You excited to get out of the city?"

I hate it when Mom calls me that. I finish texting Daniel—*these may be the last words you ever get from me*—and look out the car window. Miles of forests and pastures spread out in every direction. I used to love seeing this. Now, it looks lonely to me—everything so far away from everything else.

"Yeah," I say as quietly as possible, but the truth is I'm nervous. I imagined my first summer as a teenager would be different than this. I haven't visited my aunt and uncle's house since Uncle Lou died two years ago. Not since his memorial, when things got worse.

"Remember, Sasha, you love it here! All these trees and meadows? Maybe you and Aunt Ruthie can catch frogs at the pond! This place really filled your bucket." She's always saying stuff like this to me. I know it's part of her job as a social worker, but I don't really feel like *filling my bucket* with anything here—especially frogs. "I know it will be hard without your uncle Lou. You two were so similar." She goes silent for a minute before continuing, "But you'll see. The forest, the trees—it used to be your happy place."

I know she's right. *It used to be.* But since Uncle Lou died, I try not to think about this place. Uncle Lou spent as much time as he could outside. For him, nature was safe. He took me fishing, taught me how to make wood carvings and skip stones. When the world felt too big, he always understood. Uncle Lou knew what it was like to see and feel *too* much. He called my sensitivity a "gift"—the way I could see and hear even the quietest of animals hiding in their knotholes or the beat of the woodpeckers in the trees, and sometimes, if I was quiet and still enough, the slimiest salamanders in the pond would swim right into my hand.

But the things that make me happy just aren't the same anymore. My worlds are the ones I create on the computer with my friends. I don't want to catch frogs anymore, or cook anything. What if a month at Aunt Ruthie's feels like a year? My skin prickles. So many things are about to change.

"I know four weeks sounds long, but it'll go by fast," Mom says. "Remember that Aunt Ruthie is getting older." She pauses. "Be polite and do all the chores she asks you to do, okay? We will check in with her as often as we can."

She turns the radio down just a bit. "You know, we think it would be great if she moved back to the city with us."

"Aunt Ruthie? You mean like in our apartment? Seriously, Mom? I can't picture it," I say.

"Well, keep an eye out for her, okay? She's tough, but everyone needs a little help sometimes. Talk to her about it, if it comes up. I know that's not why you're going, and really, I want you to just enjoy everything. Play at the pond like you used to." *Play at the pond?* I'm not a baby. "And—" I already know what she's going to say, so I cut her off.

"And don't use any devices?" I say in my most sarcastic voice.

"Right," she says. I see her eyes flit over to look at me in the rearview mirror. "But it's not like screen time will be gone forever. It's about finding balance. Dr. W says this summer should help."

I trust Dr. W, but will a whole month away really help? I don't understand why I can't try to make these changes *with* my friends rather than without them. Daniel's going to be leveling up, basically getting all the best stuff in every game, and I'm going to miss out. I'll be so far behind when I get back. What if he moves on to some other game? I won't even be able to check notifications or game status. I probably can't even communicate with him. And Daniel is pretty much the only friend I have. The thought makes my hands get a little sweaty, cold. What if "getting away from it all" makes things worse?

2

I lean my head against the glass. My breath clouds the window. I listen to the hum of tires on pavement, the world speeding by in a blur. Cows graze in fields alongside hills spotted with barns. A tree-covered hill rises up through wisps of fog, and I think about what it was like the last time I came here. That trip was when I first found myself in the Gray.

We drove up here for Uncle Lou's memorial two years ago. My aunt and uncle's house is usually cozy, like a fire is blazing in the fireplace and everyone is snuggled under a blanket of warmth. That day, the house felt cold—empty, even though it was full of people. Family I'd never met. People I didn't know came up to me, the low hum of their words stuffing my head with too many voices asking too many questions that I couldn't answer. I just wanted everyone to get away from me.

Then I saw a man I didn't know holding Uncle Lou's favorite walking stick—the one with the horse head on it. It looked to me like he was trying to take it. I went up to him and told him he couldn't have it, snatching it right out of his hands. He yelled something at me, and things began to change after that. It got hard to breathe. I ran to the door, through the grabbing hands of all the grown-ups reaching for me. Everyone was trying to talk to me, but all I could hear was the sound of my heart beating in my ears. I burst through the door and out into the misty forest. When I turned around, everything looked different. The trees seemed to grow longer, spreading over the house, their branches like the arms of faceless giants reaching into the sky. A gray fog clouded over everything. I waved my hands, but I couldn't clear it away. People poured out of the faded house, the front door like a mouth opening wide. But they didn't look like themselves. They were shadows of people, like the ghosts in the stories Uncle Lou used to tell me, tall and wispy, like dark-suited tree trunks. The world was swirling. I felt off balance, queasy, like I might flip upside down. The next thing I remember was Aunt Ruthie sitting with me on the porch in the moonlight. She was holding the horse-head walking stick while I shivered in the cool air, my stomach tied in knots.

"The house, the forest, they were different," I whispered, my teeth still chattering. "So cold and gray." Even though this must have been the hardest day of her life, she put her arm around me and squeezed.

"I understand." She sighed. "Today everything is a little colder. Everything feels swallowed up in the Gray."

I've called it that ever since.

● ● ● ● ● ●

My heart beats a little bit faster at this memory as the car rounds a big curve. I exhale. We're getting closer to their house. I look out the window at the forest as we speed by it. On one of the lower hills, two horses gallop through a meadow. One is dark brown, its wild mane flying in the wind. The other is smaller, the color of tree bark, but you can tell it's strong. Its legs push the ground away as it tries to keep up. It looks like they're running faster than the car. I imagine the sound of their thumping hooves echoing my heartbeat.

3

Finally, things begin to look familiar. We pass the huge horse ranch, the long pastures spread out against the hills, and turn up the gravel road. I see places I know, small clearings and creeks we used to visit. I imagine the crunch of leaves under my feet. I see deer spring into the trees and disappear. It's like the forest wants me to remember it. I think about taking a picture. I grab my phone, but it just reminds me that somewhere, Daniel is playing Earthforge and *I* can't. I can't for a whole month. No computer. No video games except on my phone. My server will be annihilated by the time I get back. Everything I built—gone. I look at my phone, the screen looking as empty as I feel.

Mom rolls down her window as we drive up the gravel road and takes a deep breath.

"The air here is wonderful! Get outside as much as you can," she says. To me, the air smells like manure. "You know, Aunt Ruthie would go to the ranch if you asked. Maybe you'll spend time with the horses? Remember Dr. W talked about this. Horses are amazing. Being with them could be helpful."

"Okay," I say. Everyone has different ideas about what they think will help me.

"And Sasha," Mom says, leaning in even more to her professional, social worker voice. I recognize it from going to work with her sometimes. She uses it when things need to get serious. "Remember, if things get tough—try using the 5-4-3-2-1 grounding technique."

I sigh. There are so many things to remember. The 5-4-3-2-1 technique is the newest thing we've been working on. It's supposed to help me when I feel the most out of control.

"Please, Sasha," Mom says. "Please promise me you'll try?" Her voice sounds so tired, like it sometimes does after a long day of work. I think about how even on those long days, she always makes time to help me—does everything she can. I nod, then pull a folded index card out of my pocket. We worked together to write it all down on the card. I stare at it, trying to remember everything.

Breathe deep.

5—LOOK: Look around for five things you can see and say them out loud. Keep it simple.

4—FEEL: Pay attention to your body and think of four things you can feel and say them out loud. Don't make it up, just feel what you feel: your socks, the soft chair, whatever else.

3—LISTEN: Listen for three sounds. Maybe the sound of traffic outside, the sound of someone typing, or the sound of a power-up in a video game. Say the three things out loud. (If listening is possible—if not, try to remember some sounds.)

2—SMELL: Say two things you can smell. Move and find something if you have to . . . If you can't smell anything at the moment or you can't move, then name your two favorite smells.

1—TASTE: Say one thing you can taste. Maybe it's toothpaste from brushing your teeth, or pizza from the corner shop. If you can't taste anything, then say your favorite thing to taste.

Take another deep belly breath.

I show her the card. "See!" I say, holding it up. I can tell she wants to say something else, but she smiles instead, letting tears flow down her cheeks.

"Almost there," she says.

● ● ● ● ● ●

My mom isn't afraid to show how she feels. But my dad likes to keep things private. He thinks I should take more responsibility. I'm thirteen now, and it's supposed to be a time of big changes.

"You don't have to play video games *all* the time," he says. "Why don't we go hit a baseball in the park? Get outside and off those devices." I know he's just trying to help. I know as an engineer he's always trying to figure out how things work, how he can take them apart and put them back together—including me. When I was little, when the world got "too big" or I was teased about my name, all I could do was sit by myself with eyes full of tears. My name is special—from my great-grandfather, who came all the way to America by way of Ellis Island to start a new life. But people don't always care about other people's stories, so they just make fun of them. My dad had a way of scooping me up in his arms so I felt safe again.

But it seems like now that I'm a bit older, he doesn't know how to help me. I know I'm hard to help. Most of the time, at school, I look and behave like every other kid. But inside, I have too much going on. I see and feel everything around me—the people walking from class to class, the bells ringing, the clicking of keyboards, the shouting in the cafeteria.

Sometimes it's all too much.

It was when my friends and I started playing and creating video games that things got a lot better. It helped the world feel more in control. At least for a while. But everything also got a lot more complicated.

4

I'd been friends with Daniel, Nicky, and Jeremy since pre-school. The four of us did everything together. I could be myself with them. When other kids teased me for talking too much or not at all, or just spacing out, they stuck up for me. Every time. They believed in me—even when I just needed to be alone in a quiet place.

But at the beginning of the year, Nicky's family moved to Michigan to be near his grandmother, so the only way we could see each other was online—which was good for gaming, but it meant *more* hours on the computer. Then one day, out of nowhere, like he got abducted by aliens, Jeremy stopped being friends with us. We don't know why. Maybe he got tired of us? My mom says that sometimes this kind of thing just happens in middle school. After a while, Daniel and I started seeing him in the cafeteria with a new group of friends. Every time we tried to talk to him, he turned his head and pretended he didn't hear us.

Then we had a tough algebra test. Sometimes tests make me super anxious. *This* test gave me an actual anxiety attack.

I had trouble breathing. The classroom kept swirling in and out of focus. I felt like I might faint in front of everyone. I thought I might even go into the Gray.

Mr. Siqueiros helped me stand up. Daniel walked with me over to the nurse's office. I drank some water and rested, and soon I felt better.

It was later that day, when I was getting ready to go home, trying to fit my massive algebra book into my backpack, that I heard a small group of kids making fun of me, pretending to cry. "You okay? Is that book too big? You're just trying to get out of the test!" they said, all smirking. "Want us to carry your books?"

I knew they weren't going to back down; I was used to it. Bullies have a way of talking—their words stretched rubber band–thin and ready to snap at any moment. Only this time, one voice sounded different. Familiar.

Jeremy was there, too.

Hearing his voice was like a punch to my gut, and I felt tears I knew I couldn't hold back. He'd stopped hanging out with us, but this?

He looked at the other kids then back at me. He hesitated for a second, like maybe he was undecided. Maybe he was remembering that we were actually friends. But it didn't last.

"Crybaby," he said, his face twisted into shadow. "You're such a crybaby."

5

Mom says something about strawberries, and suddenly we are pulling off onto a dirt road on the edge of a wide meadow where tables are filled with fresh fruit. Gold melons and bright red berries fill baskets along folding tables. She buys a few baskets.

"For Aunt Ruthie," she says, putting the baskets in the trunk, then handing one to me. I eat a berry, and it's so good I grab another. It tastes different—like a strawberry, but with something extra.

"They're fresh," she says, "different than what we're used to in the city." She's right. I look out at the wide field as we drive off. This is definitely not the city anymore. There's so much space, so much air, and I know I should feel relieved, or refreshed, but I can't shake what happened with Jeremy.

I remember how Jeremy and the other kids pressed closer, their words crowding my air, covering me like a thick blanket. It was hard to breathe. I tried to back away. I dropped my backpack and held up my algebra book like a shield. I felt their bodies pressing against it. In my mind,

I heard the voice of Dr. W telling me *to stay calm and breathe—to imagine a peaceful scene.* I saw my mom, and I thought of Uncle Lou and skipping stones on the pond. But the kids' voices were way too loud, and by then the hallway was darkening with the shapes of other kids. I tried not to get more upset, but I could feel it, the Gray. I held it back the best I could. I didn't want it to happen here in front of everyone. My breath got shorter, and the twisting inside me ached, turning my fear into something else. Anger.

"Crybaby," Jeremy said again, and that was when something snapped in me.

I needed space. I heard my dad's voice loudest of all. *Be tough. You don't have to take it.* I gripped my algebra book with both hands and shoved it forward with all my strength. I felt the loud *crack* of the book in my spine as it connected with Jeremy's face—a sudden rush of air between us.

I wasn't expecting what happened next.

He held his hands over his face, tripping into his new friends. I reached out, tried to help him, but it was too late. He crashed to the floor. Someone yelled so loud that teachers came running. There was blood on the floor where Jeremy fell. He touched his nose. There was blood on his fingers, too.

● ● ● ● ● ●

My parents and I had to meet with Principal Shaw. I was suspended for two days. It could have been worse, but Mr.

Siqueiros stuck up for me—he told them that the kids cornered me. My parents promised that we would be "working on it." But I wasn't even sure what that meant. Working on not getting bullied? On not getting teased by people who were supposed to be my friends?

On the way home from school, Dad said he understood why I did what I did. "It's okay, Sasha. Sometimes you've got to stand up for yourself. Sometimes when everything is on fire all around you, the only thing you can do is run through it. You've got nothing to be ashamed of." But I felt like I had everything to be ashamed of.

Mom took it the hardest. When she called Dr. Winters, he suggested we have an emergency session.

I found out Jeremy had a broken nose and a cut on the side of his head from falling—he needed seven stitches. They said the scar wouldn't show through his hair. *He* would be okay. But I wasn't. Just because they couldn't see my pain, doesn't mean it wasn't there.

6

After that, things got worse. All I wanted to do was hide under my blanket at bedtime, but that wasn't easy because that's sort of what the Gray feels like—pulling a giant blanket over my head and watching the sides of it slowly float down.

At dinner the night after I hurt Jeremy, Mom started talking a lot about how it feels for her when I go into the Gray. She says that when it happens, it's like I walk through a door into a place where she can't follow me—no matter how hard she tries. She has to wait for me on the other side of the door until I'm ready to come back out. I can't find the words, but I want her to know it's not her fault.

Dad didn't talk about it at all. Later that night, I heard them arguing in the next room. My stomach was in knots. Were they arguing about me? I heard the frustration in Dad's voice. He wants to save me. He wants to fix things. Fix me. I get it. He's an engineer—fixing things is what he does. Then, even though their voices were muffled, I heard them talking about Aunt Ruthie, that she said she'd "take me for the summer." I didn't know at the time what that meant. But hearing it made me feel worse.

Under a blanket, I tried to breathe—in, one, two . . . and out, one, two—but nothing worked. Every time I closed my eyes, I thought about all those kids standing too close, their words and bodies pressing down on me. I could see and feel everything: beads of sweat, bad breath, the smells of their lunches, Jeremy's face so close to mine. My friend had suddenly turned into something else. I could feel the tight grip of my hands around the algebra book.

Sleeping that night was hopeless. I knew I wasn't supposed to, but I got out of bed to play Earthforge, hoping to take my mind off what had happened. When I'm gaming, especially building in Earthforge, I feel the most in control. But lately, it was more the opposite—I was feeling *out* of control. And that night, things got worse.

Instead of relaxing into the game, I felt my heart beating faster, all the sounds and images swirling together. My vision narrowed, and the room filled with a familiar fog the color of wet cement. I felt for the keyboard, but my fingers just tingled against something cold. I couldn't tell what was my room and what was the game, like it was all one place. I thought I was sitting still, but my legs felt like they were running through mazes of endless terrain, tearing up the ground in every direction. Then I felt it. All of my dinner came out of me. I threw up on my keyboard and desk, and then sank onto the floor, too scared to move.

My dad found me sitting in the middle of my room, eyes wide open, soaked in sweat. He sat on the floor and put his arm around me. "Okay, son," he said, squeezing my shoulders, "time for a new plan."

The next day, I sat in a circle with my mom, dad, and Dr. W. They told me I'd be spending a month with my aunt in the country, that I needed a change of scenery. And a break from technology. They told me that forming new habits will help me. They wanted me to try a medication.

Nobody asked me what I thought about it.

I could tell it was hard for my parents. They held hands, and then they held mine. Dr. W leaned over toward me, pushed his glasses up the bridge of his nose.

"You can do this, Sasha. You are an extraordinary kid."

8

I take another deep breath and open my eyes. Aunt Ruthie's house appears. It looks exactly the same as it did the last time I was here. Uncle Lou's sculptures and carvings greet us as we come up the driveway—badgers, rabbits, foxes, and other creatures everywhere I look. I see Aunt Ruthie waving wildly from the doorway.

She and Uncle Lou moved out here long before I was born. They came to help their friend, a rabbi at Temple Adat Shalom, the smallest synagogue in upstate New York. He needed help running a sleepaway camp: Camp Akiva. Aunt Ruthie helped with theater and dance, and Uncle Lou worked as the camp director. They loved it. They thought it was important to be in nature and provide a space for kids to have a chance to learn Jewish principles and get away from it all. Camp Akiva wasn't super fancy, but it had sports, theater, dance, and even horseback riding. But eventually, as even fancier camps opened in the area, it got harder for Camp Akiva to compete. The camp was on the verge of closing down, anyway, when one summer, a young girl from town got lost near the camp and was never found. People like telling ghost stories about her. And those stories became a sort of local legend. I don't like to listen to them or any of the stories Uncle Lou would tell about the ghosts and spirits in the woods near the camp.

It was hard on the camp and the whole town. Shortly after, Camp Akiva closed for good. Uncle Lou died a few years later. That's when my parents first suggested that Aunt Ruthie come back to the city and live with us, or at least move to Florida "like every other Jewish person," but she insisted on staying. She said she didn't want to leave Uncle Lou.

● ● ● ● ● ●

"Sasha! It's about time you got here." Aunt Ruthie pulls the passenger door open and draws me into an insta-hug. Mom rolls up the window and gets out of the car. I hear the blasting horns of the *Star Wars* theme song coming from inside the house. Aunt Ruthie and I have always loved *Star Wars*. We've watched all the movies together. She loves any part with Han Solo. She's also the only person I know who has actually choreographed dances to *Star Wars* music.

Even though she's shorter than I am, she practically lifts me up with her hug. Dad says that Aunt Ruthie is one of the strongest people he knows.

"Sasha, come on!" She pulls me and Mom into the kitchen, telling us so many things at once about the town. "The synagogue is practically empty nowadays, but they're trying to make it work. They teach martial arts—actually Krav Maga—there now and rent it out to all kinds of community groups. I'll take you there." I know my dad would like this. He's always wanted me to practice Krav Maga like he does. He thinks learning self-defense will be good for me, help me feel more in control.

I look around the house. It's the same as always but also different. My heart beats faster. I feel Uncle Lou everywhere.

My aunt stops for a moment, then turns around and starts telling me everything at once. "Oh, there's so much to catch you up about—I am sure you'll want to explore the old camp. The deer are everywhere this time of year! Oh, and there's the ranch at the bottom of the hill. Maybe we'll get you signed up for a trail ride, maybe even horseback riding lessons?" She stops for a moment, searching my face. "Was that too much? Should I not have said all that?"

"I'm okay," I say. As she's talking, I realize that Aunt Ruthie is speaking to me like I'm a whole person. She always has so much to say, and sometimes I'm not even sure I'm following everything. But it's never strange to her when I get quiet. It doesn't feel as if she's waiting for me to speak. It makes me feel included, but also like she'd keep barreling on or talking to herself even if I wasn't there. Maybe I'll be able to slip away and she won't even notice.

In the kitchen, I'm distracted by the overwhelming smell of something delicious. Bread? And maybe potatoes?

"Oh! My kugel! I almost forgot. Bet you've never had potato kugel this fresh before! I make it from my own potatoes. They're so easy to grow. You just throw them in the dirt, and . . ." But she stops herself. "Okay, maybe how potatoes grow in the dirt is *not* the right topic of conversation for a thirteen-year-old boy. Tell me, are you excited to be away from your mom and dad for a month?"

I try to smile. I watch Mom, who's just brought some of my stuff inside and is heading back to the car for more. "Actually," I say, "it feels terrible."

"What's the deal, kiddo?" Aunt Ruthie flips her long black-and-gray hair—it's like the salt and pepper in the glass shakers on the counter—and then pulls the kugel out of the oven. She cuts a giant piece and fits it onto a plate. I put my phone down next to me, but not before checking it first. As I figured, there's no reception. I look up at her.

"Ahh," she says, poking at the phone.

"I wanted to, you know, stay with my friends—well, my friend Daniel—and stuff. I mean . . . it's just . . ." Mom comes back inside and puts her arm around me. I can tell she wants to say something, but Aunt Ruthie raises her hand just a little, like she's playing a Jedi mind trick, and Mom stays quiet.

"I know," Aunt Ruthie says. "Of course. You're at the age when you're just starting to have your freedom, and friends are so important now. I remember summers at your age—I spent them on the beaches in Tel Aviv or at Rockaway Beach. I get it. There's nothing like that feeling."

I want to correct her, to tell her that I actually had very different plans for my summer, but I don't say anything. I don't think Aunt Ruthie will understand how kids hang out these days.

She tells a bunch more stories, piled one on top of the other—about Brooklyn, and the Middle East, and being a young girl and how she never fit in. I usually like all her stories, but I can only manage to half listen because I'm so hungry from the long drive. I imagine using the Force to pull the plate of kugel closer.

As if it worked, she slides the plate toward me. I dig in.

"My point is," she says, "I understand what you mean, and we will do the best we can to make this a summer to remember."

It's not a question—it's an invitation. If anything, at least this summer will be a chance to get out from under my parents' ever-watchful eyes. She's right about that. But I'm not sure what the point of that is if she has no Wi-Fi or reception.

"You have a bite to eat, say goodbye to your mom, and then we'll go down to the pond and take a look around."

"Okay," I say, my mouth full of hot, melty potato goodness.

Aunt Ruthie walks off with Mom, who's running her through a list a mile long and explaining all kinds of things, from daily routines to my new medicine. Out of habit, I look at my phone, watch the swirling lines as it searches for reception, then put it down and eat the whole serving of kugel as fast as I can.

Maybe it's the kugel, or maybe it's the memories associated with this place, but I start to feel a sense of relief. It's kind of nice to be away from everything. For now. At least here, if I have an episode again, it won't happen in front of everyone, and I won't hurt anyone, even by accident.

● ● ● ● ● ●

Mom walks me out to the front yard to where a small bridge stretches over a stream of rocks. My dad loves this bridge. He points out how well it's constructed every time we see it. There are wooden foxes and carved garden gnomes everywhere—beneath the bridge, carved into tree stumps, hiding under rocks. It feels like we're being watched. A small, very realistic coyote carving is sitting near the side of the house that frames the entrance to the deepest part of the forest. The wood is chipped away near the coyote's paws.

"Sasha-bug," she says.

"*Mom!*" I say. She knows I don't like it when she calls me this, but to be honest, I don't mind so much right now. I know she's leaving, and I'm nervous. She's the one who always helps me figure things out. She's the one who stays with me when I'm lost in the Gray. For a moment, I think about begging her to take me home.

"Stay on top of your medicine, all right?"

"Okay," I say. I'm still not used to how chalky it tastes.

"And listen to Aunt Ruthie. She will look after you even if you're having a hard time."

"Got it," I say.

"And Sasha . . . ?" Mom looks at the house, then puts her hands on my shoulders and stares straight into my eyes. "You watch over her, too, okay? She's getting older and she's been alone for a while now. Dad and I are hoping she'll come back with us to the city when we pick you up. At least for a visit." She shakes her head like she's said too much already, then smiles. "But that's not why you're here, of course. Remember to stretch every morning, exercise every day, write in your journal, laugh, count to ten—slowly if you have to—and spend lots of time outside working on being present. No devices. It won't be forever, but you have to try your best!"

"Yeeesss, Mom," I say.

"Remember your box breathing most of all." She starts demonstrating it until we're practicing together—in, hold, out, hold. "Promise?"

"I promise. I think I'll be okay, Mom."

She looks at me, then tilts her head to the side. "I'm sorry Dad couldn't be here. He hopes this change will do you good."

When I hear this, it only makes my heart beat faster. I know they're trying to help me, but whenever I try to "make a change," things don't go so well. I think about what happened with Jeremy, and the way the Gray feels more real and more mysterious than ever. There are so many changes happening to me lately, and I don't feel like I have control over any of them.

"Mom, all Dad ever talks to me about lately is how I need to change. What if I don't know how to do that?"

She wraps her arms around me. "Don't worry," she says, pulling me in tighter. "He sees the world differently." Then she looks me in the eyes again. "Things weren't easy for him when he was your age." I look down, trying to picture him the same height as me. "Living as a family of immigrants was difficult. Just like your great-grandfather, his whole side of the family had to work so hard to survive. He just wants you to learn how to make it in this world." I look at our car, like he might suddenly be sitting in it. "Maybe," she says, "you can think of him as doing the best he can right now?" I nod. It doesn't feel like enough.

"Maybe that's about all we can do." She smiles. "So you just do the best *you* can. You'll find a routine before you know it. This is going to be so good for you. I know Aunt Ruthie has some fun activities lined up. She can be a little wild, but try to have fun with her and go with the flow!" She kisses my forehead, and I resist the urge I usually have to roll my eyes.

"See you in a month! Don't forget to call us as much as possible!" She kisses my forehead and heads toward the car. I watch her drive off, taking all my glorious gaming plans for the summer away with her and leaving me in what feels like the middle of nowhere, with an aunt who thinks I still entertain myself by *catching frogs*. At least she's a good cook.

9

Even though she's older now, Aunt Ruthie still seems to glide through the air like she's dancing—only maybe a little slower. She reminds me of Yoda, slow and steady but with the ability to be faster than anyone else around her.

I walk upstairs and drop my bags in my room. It's the same as I remember it. A tiny rectangle with a slanted roof, an old lamp, and a huge window that looks out into the forest. I used to love looking out this window. The way the tree branches spread out like a giant tree house for so many animals, the birds hopping from one limb to another—it's so different in the city. But I would trade it all in a heartbeat for some good Wi-Fi.

"C'mon, Sasha!" Aunt Ruthie calls. I head downstairs, and we go out the door and start down the trail, weaving through the huge maple and birch trees near the outskirts of the pond. Then she motions for me to stop, and we slowly creep up, her cane lifted, waiting for just the right moment. She's pointing at the edge of the water. I remember this—one of my favorite things to do when I was little. For a moment, I think of telling her I am too old now, but she's already crouching low, so I join in. I hear a soft croak coming from the still water, and then I see them—slimy, spotted frogs—covering the whole edge of the pond. I reach for my phone to get a picture, but by the time I get it out of my pocket, some of the frogs have plopped into the water. "Put that thing away," Aunt Ruthie whispers. "See it with your own eyes first."

I sigh and pocket my phone. Aunt Ruthie crouches down even lower. The frogs quietly croak.

Aunt Ruthie whispers, "One, two . . . three!" and we jump. The startled frogs leap into the pond, *plop plop plop* in every direction, water spraying everywhere. We watch the frogs as they swim down into the murky water. We laugh. I look up and see, across the pond, a massive stone. It looks like a giant egg, or like something from space. Moss has grown all over it—as if it's wearing a green hood. There are no other stones like this anywhere. It's so large. Perfectly round. Big enough to stand on. Completely out of place in this messy, wild pond. I can't explain it. And I don't know how else to say it: It takes my breath away every single time I see it. In this moment, though, it reminds me of Uncle Lou. He called it the Stone of Power.

"It's still here, as always," Aunt Ruthie says. We walk toward the edge of the water to look at the stone. It feels like Uncle Lou is right here with us—like we can almost see him.

"Me and Uncle Lou used to sit here and eat big bags of chips," I say. "He loved to talk while he was eating." I make chomping noises. I can still hear the crunch, followed by the low hum of his voice. *This is my anchor*, he'd say. *Whenever I've seen too much, or I need to get my feet back on the ground, I come here to the stone—it's something solid and bigger than my little life. This old stone reminds me it's never too late to be or do the thing you want. Just like the story of Akiva and the stone. You know the story, Sasha? About the shepherd without hope who thought he could never change?* Even though I'd heard the story a million times, I would say no, and he would start to tell it to me again—about how change is possible for anyone, how even the smallest drop of water can change the largest stone. He never told it exactly the same way twice.

●　●　●　●　●　●

Aunt Ruthie loops her arm through mine. "C'mon. Let's go take a closer look." We walk around the edge of the pond to the hilly side, where the moss climbs over the stone. We stand on top of the hill. From here we can see through the forest, down into the pasture, and almost all the way to the ranch, where the cows look like splotches of paint against a sea of green pasture. "Stay out of the pasture. It's not safe," she says. "Those creatures can be mean."

Beyond the cows, I see a few horses grazing near an old red barn.

We kneel, then lie down on our bellies, looking out into the water. Then we reach down with our hands, over the moss, to touch the surface of the stone, to feel its granular ridges. It's cold to the touch. "How much do you think it weighs?" I ask.

"Well, according to my calculations, about four-point-seven-one tons."

"Really?"

"No! I'm kidding. But it would take a crane to move this thing. And why would anyone ever do that?" We laugh, then feel the stone for a while, staring out at our blurry reflections in the water. In the reflection, Aunt Ruthie looks young, like someone my age. The frogs begin to peek out of the water and, just like that, I feel a calm I didn't expect.

"It's going to be okay, Sasha. Don't worry," my aunt says, as if she can read my thoughts.

"Thanks, but . . . how do you know?" I ask gently, tossing dried moss into the pond and watching it float on the surface. I think about how all my dad talked about before I left was how much he was hoping I would change. I'm thirteen—I'm changing anyway, even if I don't want to.

"Because it is. Humans change all the time. It's who we are. Change doesn't always happen the way we think it should. And that's okay." She looks up like she hears something, but then she looks right back at me. "You aren't alone. There are a lot of people who love you. Our family is tough, and you are part of that family. It's just that toughness doesn't always look the same for everybody."

I take a deep breath, thinking about how my parents must have told her about what happened at school since she's already talking about toughness. The one time I tried to be tough, I hurt someone. I want to find the courage to talk to her about that, but I can still feel the weight of the algebra book in my hands, the crack as it hit his face, so I don't say anything.

"You're tough, Aunt Ruthie. I can't even climb the rope in PE." She turns to the side, and I can tell it's not easy for her. Then, all of a sudden, she taps me with her cane.

"Listen, Sasha. We are family. Our souls are threaded together. I have you, and you have me, so you are tough as anyone. And if you need it, I can lend you some of my toughness for a while until you find your own. Do you understand?"

Even though I don't know what she means, I *feel* what she's saying in my gut, or in my *kishkes*, as Aunt Ruthie would say, so I nod.

"Good. Now let's go back for another slice of kugel. Tomorrow we can run to the store to get you what you need for your time here." We get up, and our movement scares the frogs back into the water. We watch them plop into the pond. But when we turn to walk back to the house, I see something unexpected: a dark shape beneath one of the beech trees. A big animal? Or some kind of ghost? My heartbeat speeds up.

No. There's a person standing at the side of the pond, staring right at us. For a moment, I think that only I can see them—like maybe the Gray is coming.

My breath speeds up, and my legs only want to do one thing—run.

10

"Well, hello." Aunt Ruthie steps forward, her cane raised high like a lightsaber, a wide smile across her face.

The ghost person, or whatever he is, stands perfectly still against the rippling pond and the gently swaying boughs of the beech trees. I realize that Aunt Ruthie can see him, too, so that means he's here and not just in the Gray, which means that I'm still here, too. I exhale quietly.

His hair is tightly curled and his face smudged with dirt. His muddy hands stick out of the sleeves of a thick green jacket, which looks too heavy for summer. He holds a brown paper bag, stuffed full—almost to bursting. On his back is a long fishing rod, strapped to him like some kind of spear. And he's tall. Taller than my father, and my father is six feet tall. His jeans are tucked into his work boots, which are planted wide in the dirt.

"So," Aunt Ruthie says firmly. "You look familiar . . . Oh! You're the boy from the ranch! Remind me of your name?" The ghost looks at her, then shifts his eyes to me, and that's when I see he's young. But he's bigger than any grown-up

I know, except maybe my cousin Eddie, who used to play football for the Giants, but his face is young—he looks a little older than me, maybe.

Aunt Ruthie takes another step closer. "Ah, I see: a quiet soul. I appreciate the value of silence, young man. The Stone of Power appreciates it, too."

"Eli," he grunts, barely moving his lips.

"Eli? Eli," she says resolutely. "Of course. Well, I haven't seen you in an age, and you're taller than ever. What brings you out here to the Stone of Power?" Somehow, hearing her tell a stranger the name of this thing—this place that only we talk about—feels weird, and almost embarrassing. I look away.

Eli looks at the stone and then back at us. Then, without another word, he slowly walks past with a half smile on his face.

"Oh," Aunt Ruthie says, "this is Sasha." She says this like it's need-to-know information. Eli stops and looks back, then nods. He trudges up the small hill, one boot at a time, to the top of the stone. He sits down where we had been sitting just minutes before and unpacks his lunch, not looking at us again—even as Aunt Ruthie says, "So good to see you, Eli. Enjoy every bit of that lunch!"

We turn and walk on—as if that encounter was the most normal thing in the world. I hear the frogs croaking near the pond.

11

Aunt Ruthie's house is, as my father says, *rustic*—which makes sense, because it's somewhere between *rust* and *ick*. *She has everything she needs but nothing she doesn't,* as he says. In small frames on the wall along the stairs, fading photographs still shine with images from her days of acting and dancing in New York. Fancy costumes and bright stage sets. Sometimes it feels as if the first part of her life is completely separate from the second part. Except when she plays old music and dances around the kitchen.

I know I should feel safe here. Most kids would be bored right away in all this quiet, but it makes me feel a little uneasy. Even in this small room with a tiny lamp, no Wi-Fi, and an old TV that doesn't have a remote, and with the forest outside my window filled with a million wild animals from this world and who knows what else.

It's so quiet, I can't sleep. I want to play Earthforge, or any other game. I want to watch YouTube. I think about texting Daniel, but why? What would I say? Besides, since the signal goes in and out, maybe I won't be able to talk to him at all? I look at my phone: nothing. I text him: *There's no signal.* The message fails. I feel off-center, like I can't find my balance even though I'm lying in bed. I stare out the window into the trees.

Routine helps me, but there is no routine here, at least not yet. This makes it even harder to fall asleep. I don't know what we are doing tomorrow, and that makes me nervous. The trees sway outside my window, which makes it seem like the room is moving, too. It feels like I'm standing on the edge of a high cliff and looking down. I feel dizzy. I think about the summer, this next month, and the days, so many days, pile up in my mind. I breathe deeply, trying to let sleepiness finds its way in. Halfway between asleep and awake, I'm startled by a fluttering at my window. Something is bumping against the glass. Am I imagining this?

I stand up and walk to the window. It feels like I'm float-walking. Everything is thin, as if the walls are made of paper I can just push through. I look out the window and down toward the creek. The water is running quickly, gleaming under a bright moon. The glass of the window is cold on my fingertips. Then something moves through the trees. Something fast. The sky tinges gray. Through the open window, I smell wet earth, and I can hear the sound of a stream in the dark. The trees are creaking, and some-where far away I hear howling. I close my eyes and count my breaths. Eventually I feel my feet press into the floor, and the warmth of the room comes back to me a little at a time.

I sit on the bed and take more deep breaths, remembering my box breathing. I slowly exhale, pushing all the air out of my lungs. Then I slowly inhale, holding my breath at the top. Then I exhale again, doing this over and over until I can see clearly through the window glass, to the trees outside, and the room fully regains its shape, my old crayon drawings anchored to the wall.

"Sasha?" Aunt Ruthie's low voice is at the door, and I jump back into bed. She walks in holding a steaming cup of something.

"Did you remember to take your medicine?" My medicine. I forgot! I reach over to the nightstand and take it with just one gulp of water. I'm getting better at swallowing the pill each time I take it.

Without her makeup, Aunt Ruthie looks both twice as old and twice as young? Like beneath her wrinkles is another person living a whole other life at the same time. She sees me looking.

"I took off my face." She laughs. I laugh, too, maybe because it's late and we are both tired. But I notice that she seems a little more serious than usual. Maybe even sad. Whatever it is, though, she shakes it off. "So tomorrow, how about we have ice cream for breakfast! I'm taking you to town—and we can get all the supplies a young man needs. How does that sound?"

I smile. Ice cream makes everything better. Then, almost as if she can read my mind, like maybe she *is* a Jedi, she walks over and grabs my hand.

"Don't worry. I know that routine helps, so we'll get that going soon enough. I promise. I have a big surprise planned for tomorrow. After ice cream."

12

I peel my eyes open. It feels like I just slept for a thousand years. I reach for my phone. I'm supposed to try not to look at it or text my friends, I know that, but old habits die hard.

I smell bread baking. I get up and start to make my way downstairs.

"Oh good," Aunt Ruthie says when she sees me. She's spreading jam on a hot biscuit. "We need our strength for Jake's Horse Ranch, so eat up."

"Horses? Like riding?"

"Trail rides. I don't think you've gone since you were little. I can't think of a better way to start your time here."

I fill my mouth with biscuits. They're warm, and the jam is sweet.

"Oh," she says, "and we will start every morning with breakfast. I thought we could begin with that, and then see how the routine builds itself?" I nod. But it's already making me nervous that she said we would be having ice cream for breakfast, which I thought meant we were going to town, and now plans seem to have changed? And I thought a routine was something people gave me. Not something I build for myself. I kind of like the idea of building my own routine, but I still feel unsettled. I finish my biscuit, then Aunt Ruthie brings out a metal tin and unscrews the top.

"Just as I promised," she says. "Ice cream for breakfast! Not every morning, but let's start things out right." She scoops out a big chunk, vanilla with chocolate pieces, home-made. It tastes creamy and not too sweet. When it hits my tongue, it reminds me of all the time I've spent here before. It feels good. She eats a small bowl, too. "When you're done, put on some jeans. And I found a pair of Lou's old boots. They should fit." She points to my uncle's hiking boots with the worn rubber bottoms. The torn laces spilling out every-where. I always wished I could have boots like his. I never thought that I might actually be big enough to wear them.

I finish breakfast—including every drop of ice cream—then go change. I slide on the boots, which seem to fit okay, and then we get in her truck and drive down the road to the ranch.

The last time I rode a horse, I was five. Except it wasn't really a horse, it was a pony named Gus, and I didn't really ride him. Someone plopped me on his back, and he just started walking. I cried the whole time and got sunburned so badly that I barfed on my shoes when they finally helped me down.

"We used to bring the campers here for trail rides.

There's an old trail that runs right into the camp. It was my absolute favorite part of summer." Aunt Ruthie sounds like she's reading the last part of a bedtime story or a fairy tale. "There's something about horseback riding. You know horses can sense your emotions? They know if you're happy or scared, and you don't have to say anything at all. They just know. You can't hide from a horse, so you have to learn to trust each other. Horseback riding is good for the soul."

But everything she's saying just makes me anxious. Routines? Ice cream? Horses? What's next? What if it's not good for *my* soul? I think Earthforge would be better for me than all this stuff combined.

Aunt Ruthie parks the truck in a grass field in front of an enormous barn with a loft that opens like a giant yawn at the very top. On both sides are spacious pens that reach out into the pastures, spreading all the way to the forest beyond. Kids line up near picnic benches with cowboy boots and hats. They all look a little uncomfortable. Or maybe that's just how *I* feel.

Suddenly, we hear a loud whinny from far away on top of the hill. I see a horse moving like a storm through the meadow, its silvery coat and long black mane flying in the wind behind it. A giant man wearing a jean jacket and backward baseball cap walks up to us.

"Don't worry," he says. "That's one of our younger horses. She's still pretty wild. Around here, we call her the Gray. She's not a trail horse. Not yet."

Did he just say *the Gray*? How could that be? My lungs feel like all the air has suddenly been sucked out of them. I look deep into the blue sky, pulling air back in.

"Jake, this is my nephew I was telling you about. This is Sasha," Aunt Ruthie says.

"I'm Jake. Very nice to meet you." I shake his hand, firm, like my dad taught me. I smile like I'm supposed to, but my eyes are fixed on the horse galloping through the fields until it disappears. "Remember, Sasha, your backside might need a little extra time tomorrow to recover."

He laughs, but I don't.

Aunt Ruthie pokes me in the side as we walk toward the crowd. One by one, horses are led out of the barn. Beautiful and different-colored beasts calmly step out to a hitching post, lining up in no particular order. Jake turns to talk to everyone.

"How many of you have been on a horse before?" Almost everyone raises their hand. I do, too, so I won't look stupid, even though technically Gus was a pony, and it wasn't much of a ride.

He holds up a map. "Well, we have a bunch of experienced riders today, don't we, and for you beginners, I promise you the horses know the trails better than any of us. We have trails that lead all the way out to Far Point Meadow, but I think we will stay a little more local. Everyone stay with your guide, and you'll be just fine."

Just fine? Uncle Lou's old boots are suddenly a little too tight.

After a few minutes, Jake walks over to us. "All right, Ruthie," he says. "Warrior is all ready for you." She smiles.

"Sasha, we've got you on old Duke. You've got nothing to worry about. Duke knows all these trails by heart." Old Duke is the biggest horse I've ever seen, brown with giant eyes and a white star shape in the middle of his forehead. Duke is ten times bigger than Gus was, and they even have to help me get up onto his back.

I shift and adjust myself in the saddle. I let my legs stretch, getting used to the feeling of Duke beneath me. I expect to feel more nervous, for my heartbeat to speed up. I wait for the feelings to take over. I look around at the wide hills, and the forest, and the pastures that wind toward town. I feel the breeze on my face, but the anxious feelings don't come. I hear Aunt Ruthie's loud laughter as she rides up next to me. She looks tiny on Warrior, a huge white horse with dark spots and a long white mane.

"This is Warrior. He's an Appaloosa." She hugs his neck. "He's my favorite horse in the world."

Jake gives us directions. "Remember to talk to the horses. Let them hear your voice. Horses will feel you if you take the time to connect with them." I look around, and some of the other kids seem to be trying it—leaning in close, talking to their horses. But I don't know what to say. I hold the reins tightly because Duke keeps putting his head down. "Um, hi, Duke," I whisper into his twitching ear. No response. "Usually, I'm pretty nervous about stuff like this, Duke, so thanks for being so calm. One time I

45

had to ride a pony named Gus and . . ." Duke starts moving forward, following the other horses, and I'm too nervous to talk anymore.

We start off in the big pen riding in long circles, practicing with the reins, learning to lean back. It actually does feel good. Duke walks in a rhythm that feels like I'm walking, too, like it's all one movement. It's like the feeling at the end of a long day when my body is so tired, I can barely move. It feels like that, only I'm not tired. I think I might actually be relaxed? My mom always tells me to relax, and usually I just say *You relax* back to her, because I never know what she means. Maybe this is it.

After a while, we leave the pen and ride single file onto the trail through the pasture. We pass winding streams and small ponds. We see a muskrat at the edge of one of the ponds and Duke looks straight at him. They are probably talking to each other. Maybe all the creatures out here know it's good to talk to horses.

We walk on, and I feel my body sink deeper into the saddle as I get used to Duke's stride. Then from way up ahead, I hear the guide say something about going a little faster. I sit up a bit, and not long after, a whistle pierces the air. Duke's body rises a little and his muscles get tighter. Someone else shouts, "Here we go," and suddenly Warrior is going fast in front of us, trotting through the pasture. Aunt Ruthie is flying effortlessly up and down, laughing. What if she falls off? I start to see it in my mind.

What if I fall off? My breath gets shallow. My mind begins to wander.

In Earthforge, you can ride a horse—virtually. They are easy to control if you just spawn a digital carrot and feed it to them. The controls are simple, and I feel the keyboard on my fingers like I'm in the game, but then Duke starts to trot, and as I bump along with each step, I'm reminded that this is not a virtual world.

"I'm not ready for this," I say out loud. I try to hold on, but the reins slip from my hands and brush my legs as they fall. Everything is moving too fast. My eyes start to blur, and the green-and-blue world slips away. I grip the saddle horn as hard as I can. I think I yell, but I'm not sure because everything is turning gray.

For a moment, I feel like I'm floating, until, *thump*, my body crashes to the ground.

I look up—there's nobody around me. A quiet breeze blows over the pasture. I try to catch my breath. Something slithers nearby, a snakelike thing with yellow eyes, its mouth gaping like it might swallow me in one bite. But instead, it just slides back into the meadow. I put my hands on my chest. In the field it sounds like the grasshoppers are growling and the trickling water in the ponds is a waterfall—everything bigger and more than itself. I close my eyes and breathe in through my nose—one, two—and out—three, four—and slowly open my eyes, but it's still gray. Except there is something else here. A shape moving toward me.

A ghost? A person. I try to crawl backward. But then I hear a muffled voice and feel a hand in mine. Something cold, maybe wet, hits my face, and I close my eyes. When they open, my head is flooded with sound.

It's the kid from yesterday. Eli, I think, his dark curly hair full of dirt and hay. I sit up, my face dripping, and he steps out of the way.

"Are you all right, Sasha?" It's Aunt Ruthie. She's next to me. "Do you want me to pour some *more* water on you?" She doesn't wait for me to answer. She opens her canteen and pours the water until my hair is completely soaked.

"I'm okay. I'm okay." Water drips over my face. There are people and horses all around me. I feel sore and confused, and my stomach hurts badly. It often hurts when I come back from the Gray. I slowly get up. A few people clap. I notice Eli through the crowd walking away. I'm used to grown-ups seeing this happen to me, but it's always hard when kids are around. I'm sure they don't understand.

Duke is eating grass near the trail. I step over to him and put my hand on his neck. Even though my body is shaking a little, I know it wasn't Duke's fault. I also know that it's easier if I act like everything's all right. When hard things happen, Dad usually tells me to *shake it off*. I don't like when he says this, but people usually stop staring at me if I appear like everything's fine or make a joke about myself.

"Here, give him this." Jake hands me an apple. "Hold it flat in your palm. Let old Duke know you're okay." I hold the apple out to Duke. In Earthforge, when I give my horse the carrot, it just disappears. This is way messier. He chomps it, showing his big yellow teeth. Then I whisper to Duke so nobody else hears me. "What about me? Do I get an apple?"

"He's smiling at ya," Aunt Ruthie says. "You okay, kiddo?"

I nod.

"You know you have to get right back on?"

But I don't want to.

Aunt Ruthie gets up on Warrior again and leans over in my direction. "If you don't want to, that's perfectly fine, but you have to eventually. Getting back on the horse is something you'll always have to do."

"All right, Duke," I say. "Can we try again?" I put my foot in the stirrup, trying to do it myself this time. Duke stays steady at first, but right as I almost get myself all the way up, something moves in the tall grass near the stream. Duke lurches forward and I feel my leg stretching. I take my foot out of the stirrup. I don't think I can get back on yet.

Aunt Ruthie is looking at me. "You want a drink, Duke?" I say. I lead him over to the stream, and he lowers his head and takes a deep drink. Warrior appears alongside Duke and gets a drink, too. They make some horse noises—probably talking about me. Aunt Ruthie touches my shoulder, and I shake my head.

"I can't do it today. I'm sorry," I say.

She smiles and pulls Warrior's reins up lightly. Together

we walk back along the trail, Aunt Ruthie on top of Warrior telling me stories about Camp Akiva and different campers she remembers, and me walking slowly in Duke's shadow. I think about Gus. I wonder if this counts as even riding at all. Duke nudges my shoulder with his giant muzzle, maybe trying to tell me that this time it's different. I did ride him; I was up there for a while, anyway. And somehow, I know I will ride him again.

13

I feel different the next morning. Maybe a little braver? I had a dream about riding Duke into the mountains and through a meadow, and then into the now empty Camp Akiva. It was peaceful—the first good dream I've had in a long time. Usually, I log in to my computer first thing in the morning to see who's online. Today, I lie in bed looking at the forest through my window. Everything looks so different in the light. Two tiny birds chirp loudly at each other, making the bright green leaves shake. I sit up, and even though in my dream I felt like the best horseback rider ever, my body feels different. In reality, my legs are so sore they feel like they are still gripping the saddle. I try to stretch them a little and then waddle downstairs.

I wonder if I really am braver today? I think about Camp Akiva and all the time I spent with Uncle Lou exploring the forest, finding fox dens in the hollowed-out beech trees, or sailing model boats on the lake. And even though he saw strange things sometimes, he always made me feel safe. It'll be hard to go there without him, but maybe it would be fun to explore a little bit.

"Good morning," Aunt Ruthie says, pouring milk into a big bowl of oatmeal. It smells like brown sugar and honey.

"Aunt Ruthie, I was thinking about exploring the old camp today. Do you think it's safe to walk over there?"

She stares at her steaming bowl.

"Aunt Ruthie?" It's like she doesn't hear me, even though I'm right next to her.

She looks up at last. "Yes. Yes, of course. But be careful. Stay on the trails. The people who bought the land still haven't done a thing with it. The buildings are getting old. Chipped paint and broken glass, the fields torn up. I know lots of kids from the town still go down to the dock sometimes and do who knows what in the cabins. At least someone still makes use of the place. Just be careful, that's all."

"Oh, and watch out for the ghost!" She smiles when she says this, but it doesn't sound funny to me.

"Did you say *ghost*?" My voice cracks a bit.

"Oh, I'm sorry, Sasha." She looks right at me. "It's not what you think. Ghosts aren't always scary things— sometimes they can even just be memories. I only know of one real ghost. She was the sweetest girl, so I wouldn't be afraid. Her name was Miriam. They called her 'the lost girl.' She loved animals. She was always visiting the raccoons at the camp and feeding the deer in the meadows. They say she was trying to help one of them when she disappeared."

Aunt Ruthie is quiet for a while, and I don't know what to say.

"Sorry, Aunt Ruthie," I offer.

"Oh, it's okay. I miss it, you know?" She stands up a little taller and points to the photographs on the walls. "The camp was our home. Hundreds of Shabbats. Thousands of baseball games. Canoe trips. And the musicals, of course. So much joy. That much happiness would surely leave some ghosts behind."

Aunt Ruthie was the musical director of the camp for years. We used to watch the videos on her old TV, and although they always looked ancient to me, her shows seemed legendary, everyone smiling, dancing, taking bows—the crowd always on their feet.

After breakfast, I grab one of Uncle Lou's walking sticks. There's a huge collection that he carved himself. My favorite is the one that hangs on the wall. If you turn the horse's head just right, it clicks, and you can pull out a sword from the center. He used to let me play with it when nobody else was around. But it seems weird to take it down, and Aunt Ruthie would *never* let me use a sword, so I choose the one with the duck head instead.

The camp is at the end of the long dirt road—about one mile from Aunt Ruthie's house. In the city, when we walk, it's block by block. Out here the houses are so far apart, forest and meadows everywhere, that it's hard to know how far I've gone. I kick rocks along the roadside as I go. Already I'm sweating from the humidity, but everything is full of color, so green and quiet. I should feel more nervous, but right now at least, it feels safe, tranquil, like nothing out here could harm me. Then, up ahead, around a long bend, something skitters across the road—fast. A dog, or maybe something else. But I keep going. Everything here seems alive. Like I'm walking into another world.

Finally, I see the turnoff for Camp Akiva. An old wooden sign marks it. It has the Star of David in the center, and then other carvings of canoes, a baseball, a person swimming, and arrows pointing in different directions. I can tell Uncle Lou carved it.

I step around the wide gate that blocks the winding gravel road that coils down to the camp and the lake. I try to hike down carefully, but I hear something in the forest—a growl, or a yelp—and it's enough to make me forget where I'm stepping. My foot lands on some loose gravel, and then I am floating, hanging in midair momentarily before dropping straight down. I fall right on my behind, the gravel spraying out from beneath me. Uncle Lou's walking stick rolls into the grass. This is not a good start. I groan, but then there's another noise. I look back. Through the gate, I see kids on bikes: a bunch of boys and a few girls, maybe a little older than I am, with backpacks on, their hair shining in the sun. They ride around me like a parade. "Ouch," one of them says. "That looks painful." But they don't stop. I hear them laughing. I'm used to this: the laughter. I've always been clumsy. Always.

"Are you okay?" One girl stops and holds out her hand. Her brown hair is streaked with green down the middle. It matches the green stripes on her shirt. Her eyes are green, too, and she's staring at me, expecting a response. I don't know what to say. Her eyes flit down the hill to her friends. "Are you okay or what?" she says.

I grab her hand and she helps me up. "Thanks," I say.

"Be careful," she says, smiling. "You must be Ruthie's nephew? The boy from the city she's always talking about?" I smile back, trying to think of what to say. But it doesn't matter because she presses down on the pedal and the bike starts to move. "Sorry, gotta go, see you later. I have to go try to stop them."

She takes off down the hill. I watch her go, and she looks back and waves before disappearing down the road.

Stop them from what? I wonder.

14

I dust myself off, then find the duck-head walking stick and swing it like a lightsaber. I look around to see where the girl went, then think about the sounds I heard before I slipped and take my time looking around. *Be brave*, I think. I walk past cabins that are all boarded up—bunks with rusted numbers and faded words in English and Hebrew. Some have glass windows, but most are broken. It's like a forgotten village. For a moment, I imagine what it's like at night. It must be scary.

Farther down, I recognize the dining hall from Aunt Ruthie's photos—all the dances and musical theater happened here—then I pass a wooden sign shaped like an arrow. It sits at the edge of a forest path that reads LAKE.

I walk along the path toward the water, where the trees thin out and a few buildings are scattered, including a wood-shop and a camp store, and there's even an old pool in the distance. Eventually, the path opens onto a wide green field with a broken backstop and rusted soccer goals on either end. Dandelion seeds blow everywhere in the breeze. Then, I freeze—I'm not alone.

The field is full of . . . cows? No, something else. My heartbeat kicks up. The creatures lift their heads, and then I realize—deer. Deer are everywhere—some with giant antlers, some grazing along the edges of the field. I stay frozen, watching. I've seen plenty of deer before, but never like this. So many in one place. And it's so quiet in the wide green field. Like I've entered another, more peaceful world.

I slowly make my way across the center of the field. Some of the deer lift their heads and watch me as I walk. I close my eyes for a moment, squeezing them tight. I want to make sure this is all real—not just something I'm imagining. I open my eyes. The deer are still here, walking quietly in the grass. Just beyond, I see lake water touching the shore and a dock reaching out into the low morning mist along the water.

It's a long dock, and there, at the very end of it, is an actual person. A tall person just standing there. He's fishing, casting his line out into the water. I hear the whir of the line. Then I see his boots. It's the kid from the pond and the trail ride. Eli. And he's singing in a deep voice, the kind of singing you do when you think nobody's listening.

I imagine walking up to him and saying, *Hi, Eli. It's me, Sasha. We met—well, we didn't meet officially, but my aunt said hello, and you helped me when I fell off a horse . . .* Ugh. I try again. *Hey, catch any fish? . . .* I'm not sure how many times I do this—imagining what I might say. Sometimes I freeze up when I try to talk to people—like I did when that girl tried to speak to me before. Sometimes I have so many things that I want to say, but it all gets jumbled up in my head, like the words swallow each other, so I don't say anything at all. It seems like such a small thing, but sometimes it's a trigger for what comes next.

My heart is pounding. I picture the words floating away and then disappearing before they reach his ears. I'm frozen again, stuck in the tree line between a meadow full of deer and the long dock. I want to do something, but the way forward suddenly opens onto a path of infinite choices—so many that I can't make even one, and the idea of taking another step becomes completely impossible. I know the Gray might be coming. I put my hand on a tree to feel the world. To ground myself.

Breathe. My stomach twists. *Breathe.* I open my eyes wide and try to focus on my surroundings. *Breathe.*

In the stillness, I see something shiny in the grass. It's small and bright green, brighter than the dandelions. I reach down to pick it up, but when I do, a sharp sting pokes my finger. It bit me! I look for blood on my finger. None. The thing hasn't moved, but I can see it better now. It's a fish the size of my thumb with a bright green stripe along its top and two shiny hooks on its bottom. A fishing lure! Maybe it's Eli's. This is the perfect reason to talk. I can give it back to him.

15

Eli is still far away, down on the dock. He's staring right at me. No, not at me. At something behind me. I hear a crashing sound and look back. The deer are startled, springing into the trees. Some of the bike kids are there, faces wild, screaming as loud as they can, riding fast and straight toward the deer. The brown-haired girl with the green streak is shouting at them to stop. So that's what she meant.

I want to get away from all this commotion. I look toward Eli. He's casting his line out, ignoring everything. I put the lure in my pocket and start to walk in the other direction, to get away from all this, toward the boathouse that's just a little farther down the path, past the dock where Eli is. I walk fast, but I'm nervous now, and my stomach is churning. I don't want to be sick in front of these kids. I hear bikes behind me and loud voices. I hear them yell, "It's the freak!" maybe to each other, or maybe to Eli? I can't be sure.

I make it to the old boathouse, where the door has been

broken off. I go in, sunlight pouring through the holes in the ceiling. I lean against the splintered and empty boat racks and take out my phone to call Aunt Ruthie. No service.

My stomach feels like it's rising up into my chest.

One by one the bikes appear, silhouetted in the mouth of the boathouse. I stay as quiet as I can, hoping they'll just pass me by. Ride away.

They don't, slowly appearing in the empty doorframe. Something tells me that they aren't here to make new friends. My heart is fluttering fast. I take the deepest breath I can. *I need to try the 5-4-3-2-1 technique. Look . . . five things I can see. Say them out loud.* "Wood, people, tree, hand, bird." *Four things I can feel. Say them out loud.* But all I can feel is my heart beating. "My heart, my heart . . . my . . ." but it's too late. They are already inside.

"Yo, what are you mumbling?" one of them says, laying his bike on its handlebars and walking forward. His hair is bright blond, his eyes cold blue. He's wearing a tank top that shows off his skinny arms. "What's up? You okay?"

I'm not okay.

"Uh, yeah," I say, pretending to text. But before I know it, they're all coming in. I'm cornered, just like in the hallway at school with Jeremy. Just like all the times before that.

"He doesn't seem okay," comes another voice, and for a moment I imagine that maybe they can help me. Maybe if I tell them I feel sick, they'll call my aunt? But I have a bad feeling, and my instincts, unfortunately, are usually right. Their laughter is the kind that whips against your skin.

I wish I was with Daniel right now, at his house back home in the city, his mom cooking Shabbat dinner and the two of us playing video games in his room. In video games, when people get mean, you can just start over or log off. I can't log out of the situation I'm in right now.

"So, you okay or what?" says the blond kid again, his voice louder.

"I don't think he is, Boon," comes a higher voice from a girl wearing oversize mirrored sunglasses. Boon walks closer. He's taller than I am, maybe older. I can see two other girls on bikes, also with big round sunglasses, hair tied back. But I don't see the girl with the green streak in her hair.

"I'm okay," I mumble. "Just tired, I guess."

But it's the wrong thing to say.

"Aw, are you tired, little boy?" Boon squawks. "Is there anything we can do to help you enjoy your time at camp?" His voice is overdramatic, but everyone behind him laughs anyway.

"What?" I ask.

"I'm Boon, the camp director. If you want to come to this camp, it'll cost you." More laughter. He even looks back to take it all in.

"Nice to meet you," I say. "I'm Sasha."

Suddenly everything quiets down.

"Sasha? What kind of name is Sasha?" He steps closer to me, like he's trying to get a better look. I can't tell if he's really asking or if he's messing with me. I know that people like to make fun of my name. Out of the corner of my eye, I see a door off its hinges—an exit. I notice the sky turning gray. *Not now*, I think. *I can't let this happen now.* My stomach lets out a roar—it's too late. Boon walks a little closer, and that's when it happens. Everything that was inside me, my entire breakfast, comes up and out—and right onto Boon's legs.

16

Boon stares at his drenched legs, and all the air seems to go out of the boathouse. Any hope of friendship or anything normal evaporates like mist. Then all at once, it's a mix of laughter, anger, and voices everywhere.

"Gross!" someone yells.

"Shut up, Ally!" Boon shouts. Someone throws him a towel. He tries to wipe off his legs. I stay bent over, not looking up. I don't want to see his face or anyone else's. This kind of sickness happens in the Gray, but this timing is the worst. Sometimes I wish I really could disappear into a place where no one else can see me.

"What the—?!" Boon yells.

A pause. Then I feel his hands on my shoulders. He shoves me, and I crash to the dusty floor.

"Are you out of your mind?!" he yells at me.

"Get 'em, Boon," says a different kid, and another, "Get him," and another, until they become one big sound I can't understand. Boon steps toward me, fists clenched. I hear my father's voice again. *Be tough, Sasha. You don't have to take it.* But the last time I listened to his voice, I ended up hurting someone, someone I cared about. I'm not good at being tough. I'm not brave like my uncle, or tough like my dad, and even when I try to be, people still get hurt.

But Boon's coming closer, smelling awful, his face red with anger, and I know that I don't have a choice. If I don't do anything, he will crush me. I stand up slowly on shaky legs, mouth dry, stomach hollow. I fold my fingers into fists.

"That's it," Boon growls. But then he stops and quickly turns his head toward the lake. Something's happened. Something's made them all stop.

"What do *you* want?" Boon calls out in the direction of the door, sounding a little nervous. The other kids slink to the side as the doorway fills with the silhouette of someone tall, a fishing pole leaning on his shoulder. Eli. He doesn't say anything. Just stands there. But it's enough.

Boon looks at me. "This isn't over. You owe me for these pants." Then he walks toward the group and gets on his bike. Eli just watches them. He still doesn't say a word.

"Not over," Boon mouths, looking back one last time before riding off.

I feel around on the ground for my phone, but I can't find it. I check my pockets and find the fishing lure.

But by the time I stand up to give it to him, Eli's gone.

17

When I get back to Aunt Ruthie's house, jazz is blaring, and she's dancing in the kitchen. I sneak past her and run upstairs as fast as possible to change. I don't want her to see my stained and dirty clothes. I take a long shower, trying to wash everything away. I quickly get dressed and rush back down, briefly stopping on the stairs when I realize I forgot my phone. But then I remember. I left it somewhere in that old boathouse. How will I get it back? How will I bring it up to Aunt Ruthie? Maybe I can look for it after we run errands?

"Ready to go to town?" Aunt Ruthie asks.

I nod. I take deep breaths, trying to put everything that just happened behind me.

Her truck is star destroyer big—taking up almost the entire lane as we drive into Hillbertsville. People wave to her and other cars honk until we finally park. We stop and talk to what seems like every person as we walk. In the city, people walk directly to where they are going without looking up. I don't know if I could live in a place like this, where everyone notices you all the time. Still, it's nice the way people smile, the way the sun shines without giant buildings in the way. We get double scoops of ice cream at the local diner. She lets me get cotton candy flavor for both scoops, even though sugar is supposed to be bad for me. Too much can cause what Dr. W calls "a roller coaster of spikes and crashes," but Aunt Ruthie doesn't say a word— even though I'm sure avoiding sugar was one of the things on Mom's list.

"How was the camp?" Aunt Ruthie finally asks, her voice cracking a little bit. I know that she was giving me time to tell her myself. I think about telling her everything that happened, but it's embarrassing, and I don't want her to worry about me getting along with other kids in town.

"I saw *a lot* of deer," I try to say in a happy way.

"Oh, yes." She stops and looks around the street before crossing. "Even when the camp was full, there were so many deer all the time. I think they know they can't be hunted there. One time your uncle Lou had to—" She suddenly stops. "Well, anyway. That's ancient history. Just like me!"

We make our way over to a bench near the hardware store and watch the cars slowly roll by. Even the cars here seem less stressed. In the city, cars honk like they're yelling at each other, but here, any honk feels like a kind hello. Near the post office I notice a little building with words in Hebrew and English on it. TEMPLE ADAT SHALOM. And just below those words is a banner with the words NATE'S GYM spray-painted in blue. In the lower corner of the banner are the letters MMA and the words KRAV MAGA.

My father does all kinds of martial arts. When I got a bit older, he started telling me about how dangerous it had been in the neighborhood where he grew up. He talks about how he "got jumped" a lot. How he had to learn how to fight just to survive. I know this is part of why he's always telling me to "be tough." He tells me that practicing martial arts helps him focus in complex situations and control his emotions, even when he thinks about his past. He's been trying to get me to try it with him ever since I was little. After what happened with Jeremy, Dr. Winters even suggested I try martial arts as a way to learn how to control my body and my feelings more, to learn discipline. My mom hates this idea. She doesn't like any kind of fighting. Sometimes my parents even argue about this. I know they both just want the best for me. I wonder what it might be like if I did learn how to have a little more control, learn how to actually defend myself? Maybe, without my dad here to look over my shoulder and watch everything I do, I could try. I bet he would be so impressed.

"Aunt Ruthie, is that a gym?"

"It's the synagogue, but these days they can barely get a minyan."

We don't go to synagogue that often, so I don't always know what all the words mean. She must sense this, because she says, "A minyan is when you have enough people to have services, and it was getting hard to find enough people, so the rabbi's son, Nathan, started teaching martial arts to kids. Maybe some Jedi training would be good for you?" I think of my mom and what she might think, but Aunt Ruthie practically pushes me off the bench. "Why don't you go check it out while I pick something up at the drugstore."

Inside the gym, kids of all ages roll around on wide blue mats, throwing punches and kicks. It looks chaotic and orderly at the same time. And there, in the corner of the gym, is Eli. Again? This time he's in a black shirt with red letters on it, and he's barefoot instead of wearing his boots. Is Eli an instructor? No, he seems to just be working out by himself. I try to find the courage to thank him for saving me, or to tell him that I found a fishing lure in the meadow that might be his. But before I can, a man wearing a karate-style outfit with a black belt tied around his waist steps in front of me.

"Hey there," he says. "I'm Nate. Welcome. You know"—he leans in like he's sharing a secret—"Imi Lichtenfeld said he invented Krav Maga so that 'one may walk in peace.' Is that something you're looking for?" I smile. It's exactly what I'm looking for.

He starts spouting off a lot of words in all directions, about martial arts, and goalsetting, and discipline. I try really hard to listen.

"So," he says. "Ready to learn how to take care of yourself?"

I nod.

Nate hands me a flyer, and then I walk out the door, back toward Aunt Ruthie, who's tapping her feet wildly, dancing to some far-off music.

I'm walking toward her, excited about Krav Maga, when I see them: Boon and the other kids walking down the sidewalk in my direction. I freeze. Do I run? Duck back into the gym? Rush across the street? But it's too late—they're already here.

"Well, look at this!" Boon walks straight up to me. "What's up, Sasha? Are you here to buy us some ice cream?"

The other kids laugh. I search their faces. I know all about bullies. I know I'm supposed to understand that they also have pain and all that, but I can't understand why they care about me. They don't even know me.

"Leave him alone, Boon." It's the girl with the green streak in her hair. She walks right up to Boon and pushes him in the shoulder.

The other kids let out an "Ooooooh."

"Let's go," Boon says. They get on their bikes, but just before he rides off, Boon stops and whispers, "Not over."

"Don't worry about him," the green-haired girl says. "He's just full of himself." She waits for them to get a little farther away, then continues, "He thinks he's the king of eighth grade. I thought you were going to punch his lights out."

"You did?"

"Yeah," she says. "I'm sorry about what happened. I was

busy trying to stop them from scaring all the deer. I hate when they do that. But I was too late. I got to the boathouse just as I *thought* you were going to attack him. I was surprised when you took it in another direction. I mean, throwing up on him was still pretty great."

I can't help but laugh.

"I'm Ivy, by the way," she says.

"Sasha."

"Yeah, I know," she says. "I like your name."

"You know my name?" I look at her, confused.

"Of course! Your aunt always talks about her nice Jewish nephew from the city. I'm surprised we've never met before. I've lived here my whole life. Whenever someone new comes around, I make sure I get to meet them."

Aunt Ruthie crosses the street and walks up to us, looking like she's seen a friendly ghost.

"Ivy Diaz! So happy to see you," she says.

"Hi, Ruthie." Ivy hugs her.

"Ivy is one of my finest dance students." She loops her arm in Ivy's and they spin around on the sidewalk.

"I gotta go, but see you later. Oh, here." She reaches into her pocket and hands me a dusty rectangular thing.

"My phone!" I shout, grabbing it, the screen completely dark. In that moment, I feel the worry I buried deep inside of me just float away into the air. I smile at Ivy.

"Sorry it's all dusty. I went back to the boathouse again after everyone left. I like walking through camp when it's quiet. I wanted to see if the deer had come back—they didn't, by the way. Your phone was sticking out from under a broken floorboard. I almost missed it."

"Thank you, Ivy!" Aunt Ruthie shouts as Ivy runs back across the street to catch up with the group of kids.

Why does she hang out with them? I wonder. She seems so nice.

Then I notice my aunt staring at me.

"You don't have to tell me anything," Aunt Ruthie says. "Unless you want to."

We head back toward the bench together, letting the sun shine on our faces.

18

Aunt Ruthie looks at the flyer in my hand. "So, you gonna learn how to punch someone's lights out?" When she says this, I feel the thud of my algebra book on Jeremy's face.

"I don't really want to punch anyone's lights out," I say. "I just want to be left alone. I'm not tough like that—not exactly normal."

"Normal? Who's normal?" She stands up and gracefully twirls around twice, as if to imaginary music. I sit down on the bench and put my head in my hands, my eyes wet from sudden tears.

"I just always feel like I make it hard for everyone around me," I say.

We sit silently for a while. Aunt Ruthie reaches into her purse and pulls out some gum, a few slips of paper, and eventually a small wood carving of a tiny creature—a little dragon coiled up. She holds it in her palm, then spins it around. It looks smooth except for the scales and teeth.

"Lou struggled every day, you know." Her voice is quiet. "And even though he got up every morning and gave the camp announcements—dressed up like a giant chicken or a superhero to make everyone laugh—it was never easy for him. He was desperately anxious every single day." She looks off into the distance like she's trying to remember something, or looking for something she forgot about. I reach out and touch her hand.

"He had to take this little mensch with him all the time just so he could focus. Sometimes he couldn't even sleep without it. He would hold it in his hand, even talk to it. Is *that* normal?" She laughed so suddenly that people on the other side of the street looked over at us. "Your uncle Lou carved and painted these little wood figures until the day he died. Is *that* normal?" She hands me the dragon carving. I run my fingers over the scales and teeth, so many small details.

"Do you ever think of leaving this place?" I ask. She shakes her head like I've said a bad word.

"It's always hard, Sasha, but it doesn't matter. I wouldn't want it any other way. I get to see him everywhere I look," she says. "I get to see his creations looking at me: his wooden foxes, gnomes all over the garden, the other, nameless whatsits down by the pond. Everything he carved had a life of its own and was part of the unique way he saw the world. He saw things other people couldn't. It scared him sometimes, but when he learned how to live with it, it actually gave him some peace. He thought that if we could see the big picture, it might just help us be better to one another. I think that's how he could run the camp. Maybe *you* need to see the things that happen to you in a different way?" She puts a finger on the wood carving. "All this makes me feel close to him. I could never leave." She coughs, takes a deep breath, and then looks around. Then she grabs the Nate's Gym flyer and shoves it into my hands. "Go sign up," she says. "There's nothing wrong with a good punch once in a while!"

19

By bedtime I am exhausted, but I'm having trouble falling asleep again. My thoughts are like a tornado. I keep thinking about Boon, and what happened with Jeremy, and all the things I'm missing out on back home. I even miss my mom's prayers before bed. I decide to text her. At first I try to tell her about how hard it is to sleep, but I don't want her to worry, so I settle on something boring—letting her know I'm okay. It doesn't send, but I can try again tomorrow when we're in town.

When I finally do fall asleep, I have one of my realistic dreams about my first day of kindergarten, the kind where it feels like I am really there again.

In the dream, I'm at one of those little tiny desks, sitting in a plastic chair. I cut my finger with some stubby scissors I was using for an art project. I remember crying, but no one came. The purple construction paper on the table in front of me began to lose its color—like the color was leaking out until it was only a gray puddle of crayon wax. Everything else in the room looked different, too. The fish in the tank in the corner of the room got bigger, like they might shatter the glass. Things got foggy. The lights, the colorful posters on the walls all faded. I was breathing hard, and I couldn't stop. My eyes stayed open. I could see everything, including the teachers coming to get me and placing me on pillows in the corner, but it was like they were just silvery figments surrounding me. Then, suddenly, color started coming back in, and sounds and words—the words of my mother, who was staring into my dry eyes.

Dr. Winters says my dreams are *super dreams*. They are good for me. He says they help me work through and understand the things that have happened. *Maybe*, he says, *they are memories trying to be let go*. That if I can learn to let go of certain things that have happened to me, they'll give me less trouble. He says lots of kids and adults go through what I am going through. This is one of the reasons that he gave me medicine to take before I left for the summer. I've never had to take medicine before. But I hope it can help me.

20

"Line up," Nate, our instructor, calls out. I scurry into the line along with a few other kids who are smaller than I am. Nate is facing us and I see that Eli is all by himself in a corner of the gym. I have the fishing lure in my gym bag. After class I can try to give it to him.

Nate says, "Kida." We bow, then start to practice punches and kicks, at first in the air, and then eventually with partners wearing pads. It feels weird, like I might trip at any moment, but it does feel good to punch. Nate teaches us to exhale when we punch. This goes well. I know all about breathing. At the end of class, we do twenty burpees. I'm the last to finish, like these smaller kids have hollow bones or something. We bow out on the sweaty mats.

"Eli," I say, wiping sweat from my face. He turns to me.

"Hi, um, so I just wanted to say thanks, you know, for helping me with the horseback riding and, um, at the camp?" He stares at me, his mouth a straight line beneath what seems like a mustache starting to grow. "You know, at the camp? Yesterday."

He raises an eyebrow. Then he shrugs and turns away.

"Also," I say, reaching into my bag and carefully pulling out the bright green fishing lure. "Is this yours?" I hold it up, avoiding the hooks. He looks at it slowly, and for the first time, something like a smile appears on his face. Then, quick as a snakebite, he snatches it from my hand.

"Where did you get this?" he snarls. I take a deep breath.

"I found it in the grass near the dock. I wanted to give it to you, but that's when Boon and everyone showed up. Is it yours?" He looks at the lure and then back at me.

"It's my little brother's. It's his favorite." He folds the lure into his sweat towel.

"Oh, good," I say. "Is he here, too?" Eli's face tightens up again, and he starts packing up the rest of his stuff. I do the same and make my way toward the door, and that's when I feel Eli's big hand on my shoulder.

"Listen," he says. "Just stay away from Boon and you'll be okay." Then he walks away.

"Good work today, Sasha," Nate calls out. "Remember to keep your hands up and recoil your punches. Strong stance!" He waves to Aunt Ruthie, who's staring at me through the window.

"Is that Eli from the forest the other day?" she says when I go outside. She's still staring through the window.

"Aunt Ruthie!" I say, trying to stop her from staring. "Yeah, he works out here."

"He seems like such a nice kid," she says. "Not like those

boys." She points at the park across the street. I see Boon there playing baseball. A crowd has gathered. Aunt Ruthie follows my gaze, then leans over. "It must be hard to be those boys. This town really roots for them. If you ask me, it's too much pressure to be famous Little Leaguers at this age," she says, and we turn away from the scene and walk back to the truck.

21

Within a few days, I start to build a routine. In the morning I have breakfast, and later in the afternoon, I go to the synagogue/gym and practice punches, kicks, and fighting stances. Sometimes I try to talk to Eli, but he's laser-focused on punching the bag.

But in between I catch frogs and salamanders in the pond. I keep them in buckets by the house, making sure they have enough water and leaves, and a rock to sit on, but today I feel like switching up my routine. I decide to hike up the other side of the hill—past the pond and the Stone of Power, up and out beyond the trees and into the wide meadow. I walk into the warmth where the grass grows tall. There are cows everywhere—like black-and-white puzzle pieces spread throughout the field. They look cute, like cartoon cows happily grazing. I feel a sudden buzz in my pocket. I pull my phone out and see tons of notifications. Missed calls, texts. A single bar fades in and out. I text my mom back right away to let her know I'm fine. There are lots of texts from Daniel, too. I scroll through every message reading about Earthforge, and different videos I need to watch. I try to open one of the links, but it just spirals. Not enough reception. Then I get to his last text: *Saw Jeremy. He got his stitches out finally. Still mean.* I try texting him back, even just one emoji, but it fails every time. I grunt in frustration, my heart racing already.

In the field the cows moo loudly. Then one of them looks up. It has horns and doesn't look like a puzzle piece at all. It snorts and locks its eyes on me. I feel my heart beating faster, my legs getting weak. The grass starts to grow taller, or maybe I'm shrinking. The bull is staring and starting to move closer. I know the trees are just behind me—if I can get to them, then I'm safe. I breathe the best I can, and I think about the Krav Maga I've been learning, but nothing I've learned so far has taught me how to handle a bull.

I try to move my legs, but they feel like they are tangled in the soaring meadow grass. For the shortest moment, my breath flutters in my chest. Colors start to fade. The bull stomps its foot, and each hoofbeat feels like it's shaking the whole pasture. The bull is suddenly bigger, a monster, its horns spiraling into the air. I feel a cool wind, and it reminds me to exhale like I'm punching, and the color floods back into the meadow. The grass lets go of me. I turn to run . . . and slip.

I fall right as I turn. I stepped in something: a cow pie, freshly made. It's splattered all over my leg. I want to stay in the grass, but I know this bull will run right over me if I do. Instead I pop back up as quickly as I can and sprint into the forest without looking back. I hear the beat of hooves behind me, feel the ground shaking. I run like I never have before, into the trees, down the hill, to the pond, all the way to the Stone of Power. I try box breathing to calm down, but the smell of the manure on my leg makes my eyes water. I want to jump into the pond to wash it all off.

Up on the hill, I see the bull in the tree line, its eyes shining into the forest. It's a regular bull again, but it still looks dangerous. It fumes there in the trees, snorting into the woods where I was just a moment before, then slowly meanders away. I sit atop the stone, my fingers pressed into the moss on its surface. I slow my breathing, trying not to smell myself, and watch the frogs swim around in the pond, their legs like scissors opening and closing. I imagine Uncle Lou coming here, the deliberate way he'd place each wood carving. Maybe there are still some here. I search for them with my eyes until I feel calm again. "That was a close one, Uncle Lou," I say to the air. The frogs croak back at me.

I slosh home in my cow poop pants, one step at a time. I go to the garden first and hose myself off as best I can. There is a bike near the front door. I recognize it, but from where? When I walk inside, I hear jazz, and the furniture in the living room has been cleared aside. Aunt Ruthie is there waving her arms back and forth, and so is Ivy! They're dancing together in the living room. When I close the door, they turn toward me, their faces immediately scrunched.

"What in the world is that smell?" Aunt Ruthie approaches me, pinching her nose. Ivy is behind her, doing the same thing.

"Sorry," I say. "I got chased by a bull in the meadow, and . . ."

"Lucky," Ivy says, her voice coming out nasally from holding her nose.

"It wasn't lucky," I say. "It was terrifying."

"No," she says. "Lucky's the name of the bull. You've never seen a bull before, have you? Be careful. He remembers faces."

Aunt Ruthie takes me into the bathroom, then hands me a stack of towels.

"Here you go. Get cleaned up. We're almost done with the lesson."

22

When I come back downstairs, Aunt Ruthie sniffs the air to make sure the smell is gone, then grabs my arm. "Sasha, will you walk Ivy out?" she says, shuffling us toward the door.

We get outside, and Ivy smiles. "She's the best, you know? I've been taking dance since I was little, and she's the most fun teacher I've ever had," Ivy says.

"Cool," I manage to say.

"I mean, there aren't exactly lots of choices here. Once, I went to visit my cousins in Newark. They all take hip-hop dancing. It's so cool. But that's the only time I've ever gone anywhere. Here we just have ballet. I always did ballet grow-ing up. But when my mom found out that Ruthie was giving modern dance lessons, she didn't want me to miss out. So, I've been going to her house for the last couple of years. She's such a good dancer." She lifts her arms suddenly and spins, then puts heavy hands on my shoulders and says, "You were once wild. Don't let them tame you."

"What does that mean?" I say.

"It's Isadora Duncan. Your aunt Ruthie knows of all the great dancers. Modern dance is wild like we are supposed to be. It helps us become who we really are!" She jumps and twirls, her feet landing softly.

"I like computers. Have you ever played Earthforge?" I say, trying to sound like I have something interesting to share, like her dancing. "I mean, I don't just like them. I like creating them, you know: building, coding, animating, and stuff."

"Animation? Like *Spirited Away*? I love Miyazaki."

"Me too! But no, more like little videos about video games. Like Kirby eating a whole planet. Or Pokémon." Ivy looks a little lost.

"You don't play video games, do you?"

"Not really," she says. "I play Minecraft at home sometimes, with my mom. She likes to build historical sites. She didn't like it when a creeper blew up a whole wing of the opera house she built, though. But no. My mom doesn't think video games are good for me. She has a lot of strong opinions."

"Do you agree with her?" I ask.

"Kind of? I mean, I would rather dance, or go down to the camp and look for the animals there, or swim in the lake. You know, spend time outside, in nature . . . you should try it."

I know she's not being mean, but I can feel myself getting upset, hollowed out. My parents are always telling me to get outside. Always. And I *am* trying. I think if Uncle Lou were here, he would tell me that, too. Now Ivy is saying the same thing.

"We have lots of nature in the city—Central Park is huge!" I retort, and Ivy smiles. "What's so great about going outside, anyway?" I continue, but as soon as the words leave my lips, I know how desperate they sound. "I'm fine doing stuff on the computer. I'm creating, expressing myself."

"Sure," Ivy says. "It just seems like its own tiny world, you know? It sucks you in."

Now she sounds like Dr. W.

"Yeah, I guess that's true. That's one of the reasons I'm here," I say.

"Maybe you're here to be friends with me!" Ivy says. She flips the green streak in her hair back dramatically. "I get it, though," she says. "I know what it's like to have a *world* you live in. My world is here. It's always been here in this small town. More than anything, I want to go to New York City, maybe see street dancers, or Broadway? I don't even care. I just know that it's my dream. Who knows, Ruthie even says that maybe one day, I could go to Juilliard!" But she gets quiet after that. I hold back one thousand questions. To me, Ivy seems like someone who could do anything. "Anyway . . ." she says, suddenly smiling, "your aunt is awesome. She at least gives us something different. Last year during . . ." Ivy holds her fingers up. "You know, with the candles, it's a holiday."

"Hanukkah?" I say.

"Yes! She had some of her students over, and we all lit the candles, and she made deep-fried potato pancakes. They were so good. I ate about a hundred of them."

"Latkes," I say.

"*So* good," she says. "You know, before that I had never even heard of Jewish food or knew anything about the holidays at all. I remember your uncle always wore the little hat?"

"A yarmulke?" I say.

"That's it! It always looked like it could fall right off," she says, pointing to the spot in her hair where the green starts.

"Why did you make your hair green?" I ask.

"I was born this way," she says, holding the colored part in her hands.

Then she starts laughing. "Just kidding. I just love the color green, and my mom told me that I've always spent a lot of my time outside, no matter what, since I was a little girl. One day, I was playing near the creek and fell into poison ivy."

"You did?" I say. "I've heard that's the worst."

"It usually is," she says. "But for some reason, nothing happened, and I was, like, rolling around in it. My mom thinks it means I've been blessed by nature. We've been putting this green streak in my hair ever since, and everyone calls me Ivy. Only a few people know my real name! It's Isabel. But don't tell anybody, okay?"

"I won't. I don't have anyone to tell, anyway."

She takes a big swig from her water bottle.

"Listen . . ." she says. "Don't worry about Boon. Just stay away from him."

"Why do you hang out with them?" I grumble.

She looks at me with cold green eyes, but then she smiles. "Who else am I gonna hang out with? They've got problems, and I don't always like how they act, but I don't know. I've just been around them forever. Small towns like this . . . we don't get to be picky about friends."

I nod. Sometimes we are friends with people just because we are. I think about Jeremy. Maybe we could have been friends again if I hadn't smashed his face with my math book. Ivy rolls her bike out toward the driveway but stops at the big green bucket full of salamanders floating like orange candies on top of the water.

"Whoa, did you collect all these little guys?" She reaches into the bucket, and right away one of the salamanders scurries up onto her finger. She lifts it up and whispers to it. "I'm gonna call you Peaches!"

"Sometimes I find them at the creek, but mostly at the pond down the trail."

"The one with the big boulder stuck into the side?" She looks up at me.

"Yeah, the Stone of . . . yeah, that one. I usually put them back around now."

"Can I come?" She lets Peaches dive back into the water.

We take turns carrying the big green bucket, water splashing out of the sides, the salamanders either attempting to hide under a piece of floating bark or riding the waves of the back-and-forth motion. When we reach the pond, the frogs dive into the water. We place the salamanders one by one into the mud leading up to the pond. We say goodbye to Peaches first. At the bottom of the bucket, the littlest one is hiding beneath the piece of bark. Ivy takes him out and says, "Awww, this one's like you: all quiet and shy." She sets it down at the edge of the pond, but it just sits there, frozen. Then suddenly, like a button got pushed, it springs up and dives into the water.

"I love this place," she says. "My grandpa said this place is definitely part of a ley line."

"A what?"

"A ley line . . . I don't know, it's like this supernatural path between places that carries energy from one mystical place to another. My family is really into all that. They say this is one of the spots on the path."

I consider the Stone of Power, and I think of Uncle Lou and all the things he liked to talk about. Then, for some reason, I think of Eli.

"Hey, do you know a kid named Eli?" I say.

She looks at me like I've said something wrong.

"It's just, he sort of helped me that day at the camp, and Boon seemed to be kind of afraid of him."

"I don't really talk to him. Nobody does. Not since . . ."

She pauses and takes a deep breath. "Look, just be smart and stay away from him, too, okay?" I have more questions I want to ask, but I can see that she's looking around, seeming a little nervous.

When we get back to the house, she warms up again. "Hey, do you want to go swimming at the camp tomorrow?" The idea makes me a little nervous. What if those other kids are there again?

"Well, I have lots of things I need to do in the morning, and I have Krav Maga class in the afternoon, so . . ."

"Hello, it's summer! We have plenty of time! I'll be there around ten. Do you have a bike?"

"I don't."

"Fine," she says. "I'll meet you here at ten." Then she rides off. I suddenly feel the dirt caked on my hands, and I think about swimming. I used to love going swimming, but I can't remember the last time I went, or if my swimsuit even fits me. Most of all I think about how maybe, just maybe, I might have made a new friend.

23

It's almost bedtime, and I'm staring at my phone. Mom texted to say she misses me, and that it's already hot and humid in the city, something I don't miss at all. I really hoped to see a text from my dad, but there's nothing. I write him a message anyway. I tell him I'm taking Krav Maga and hit send. Maybe it will go through. The comforting glow of the screen is reassuring. I know I should follow the rules and turn it off, but I don't want to just yet. Instead I play Drop the Block, which is really boring in solo mode.

Aunt Ruthie appears in the doorway, holding her tea. "So," she says. "Are you making friends with my student?"

"I think so," I say. "Ivy wants to go to the camp and swim at the dock tomorrow. Also, I didn't know you were still a teacher."

"I've been teaching dance to a few of the kids in town. People don't know how to get wild around here. It's good to let loose sometimes. That Ivy, she's got the stuff. She desperately wants to go to the city, maybe even be a professional dancer, but her mom doesn't want her to . . ." She trails off.

I start to feel tired but not exactly sleepy. Dr. W told me the medicine might do this. "Aunt Ruthie? Did Uncle Lou ever take medicine?" When I see the look on Aunt Ruthie's face, I want to take the question back.

She stares out the window. At first she looks concerned, her expression twisting into a question mark. Then she sees the medicine bottle on my nightstand and her face unwinds.

"Oh yes," she says. "It really helped him when things got a little too stressful around the camp. We had a great doctor who helped us find just what he needed."

I want to ask her what else it did to him, but instead I let out a giant yawn.

"That yawn means you are running out of air, Sasha, and you better get some sleep if you're gonna swim in the morning."

I'm so tired, but I keep having half dreams where I'm trying to swim, gasping for air. I can feel the water in my hands, the pressure of pushing against it, until I eventually fall asleep.

24

The next morning, I wait for Ivy by the road. It's still early enough for the mist to be sticking to the trees. Below a giant birch, something, some animal, is creeping low, like it's trying to hide. I can't tell what it is.

"Sasha!" Ivy calls, breaking my concentration as she pedals down the dirt road, the basket on her bike overflowing with stuff. When I look back, the animal is gone.

Ivy wants to ride double. She makes me sit on the seat of her bike while she stands up, pedaling down the gravel road toward Camp Akiva. It's bumpy. I hold on to her shoulders, which makes it hard for her to pedal. I'm not light, so I know she must be really strong. When we get to the hill, we hop off and wind our way down toward the dock, past the abandoned dance/food hall. She stops at the bunkhouses.

"Look," Ivy whispers. She points to a broken doorframe inside Bunk 12. "Did you see that?"

"See what?" I say nervously, stepping back. But I did see it. Something moved.

"Maybe," Ivy says, turning to me, "it's the lost girl." She

says it in a low, spooky voice, then laughs, but it still sends a chill through my body.

"Who?" I say, even though I know exactly who she's talking about.

"The lost girl. Her name was Miriam. People say she went out in a rowboat to rescue some animals and never returned. It was a long time ago. I've never seen her, but Boon and the other boys swear they have—a ghost roaming through the camp with a parade of raccoons and other animals behind her." Ivy steps toward the bunkhouse. I stay right behind her.

"Do you think it's true?" I whisper, trying to breathe and not let her see that I might be scared.

"Maybe," she whispers back. "All kinds of things happen all the time around here. The forests, the meadows—people say they are full of spirits and monsters."

"Monsters?" I stop. "What do you mean?"

"Didn't you meet Lucky yesterday? That's a monster if I've ever seen one."

I exhale and force out a laugh. We creep closer until we hear a faint scratching, and then they appear. A family of raccoons is moving around inside Bunk 12. When they see us, they sit on their behinds and stare right at us. We sigh in relief.

"I hope a coyote doesn't get those guys," I say as we hop back on the bike and ride slowly away.

So where's Boon today? I've been waiting to ask. I try

not to think the worst, that this could be a trap, that she's just bringing me to camp so Boon and his gang can jump me. I can't keep the thoughts from piling one on top of another. The trees begin to darken a little. Ivy keeps pedaling, and I keep holding on. If it is a trap, it's too late for me to stop it now.

"Sasha?" she says, snapping me out of my thought spiral. "You okay back there? You have to lean with me."

"Sorry," I say. "I'm okay."

Just like last time, we see Eli at the dock, his hair ruffled, his fishing rod steady in his hand, a bucket planted next to his heavy boots.

"Oh no." Ivy stops the bike. "We can't go in there right now."

"Why not?" I ask. "It's okay."

"You don't understand . . ." she says, but it's too late.

"Hey, Eli!" I call out. He looks up but quickly turns back to the lake. I hop off the bike and walk toward the dock, Ivy reluctantly following. The dock splinters out over the blue water, silent and glassy in the calm morning. Eli reels in his hook and begins packing up. "Catch anything?" I say, but I must sound silly, because the bucket is full of round, blue-and-white fish. Eli doesn't respond, picks up his bucket, leans his fishing rod against his shoulder, and walks off the dock. "See you at the gym later on?" I say.

He stops, looks back, nods, then walks on.

When he's out of sight, Ivy parks the bike in the center

of the dock. She takes our towels out of the basket, spreads them out at the very end, and sits down. I look into the water, where fish swim in and out of mossy rocks and submerged logs.

"That was close," she says quietly.

"What do you mean?" I ask.

She takes a sip of water.

"Okay, I'll tell you what I know, but it is the most supersecret story, okay? You can't repeat it to anyone, ever. Promise?"

"I promise," I say skeptically.

Ivy grabs my wrist and bends it back.

"Ouch, stop that!" I say.

"Promise?" she says.

"I promise, geez." She lets go.

"Last year, something happened." She caps her water bottle. I sit down at the edge of the dock and let my feet hang over the edge.

She scoots closer to me. "Eli is a year older than us, but he has a little brother, Jesse, who's a couple years younger than we are. They are—were—super close. Eli took him everywhere. Last summer, Eli worked a lot at the horse ranch down the road from here. He took Jesse there because his dad had to work all day, I guess, and, well . . ." She looks down into the water. Fish swirl around beneath us.

I wait.

"One day, something happened in the barn to one of

the trainers, Tommy. Some people think Jesse was playing around, teasing the horses, and Tommy got really mad and yelled at him. But some people think Eli just didn't like Tommy because he was mean to him and Jesse all the time. No one knows exactly how it started, but they got in a really big fight." She stops. Her voice gets really shaky.

"So, what happened?" I say.

"Well, that day at the barn, Jake and some of the other people at the ranch found Tommy and Eli lying unconscious on the floor. They fell out of the hayloft. Jesse was at the top of the hayloft looking down at them, crying. People say all kinds of things about what happened—nobody really knows. But what everyone does know is that after the fall, Tommy was hurt really badly. People say Eli beat him up and paralyzed him.

"Tommy's gone now. After it all happened, the police did a big investigation, and later on they arrested Tommy! But everyone still steers clear of Eli."

I'm stunned. It feels like all this is impossible, but it certainly explains how people look at Eli. How people treat him. Could Eli really be that dangerous? My mind wanders to the hallway back at school, and the feeling of all those kids pressing down on me. The same feeling I imagine Eli might have had. Would I swing that math book again if I had to? Am *I* dangerous? I look at Ivy.

"So that's why Boon is afraid of him."

Ivy nods.

"Everyone is! They think he could do anything. Before all that, Eli was on the baseball team with Boon—they were best friends. Now he has to do community service every weekend. Jesse moved to California with his mom, and Eli stayed here with his dad. My mom heard that Jesse didn't feel safe around Eli, so he and his mom planned to stay with family out there until he felt better. At the ranch, Eli would help out the younger kids and Jesse was always with him. Now, Eli is always alone, helping out with the horses at the ranch, fishing, working out at Nate's. He barely goes to school."

I don't say anything because I don't know what to say. Finally, I ask, "Why is that such a secret story? There are so many things that aren't even known. I mean, what really happened?"

"Yeah." She nods like she agrees. "I guess you're right. I think it's just that *nobody* really talks about it."

We sit in silence for a while. The lake is so blue beneath the golden sun.

"So, have you ever been to New York City?" I ask.

"No. Ruthie tells me that when I go to college, I could try to go to a performing arts school there, but my mom hates the city. Like I said, she has strong opinions," she says, tossing a pebble into the lake. We watch it *bloop* into the water. "She and Jennifer moved out here to get *away* from the city." Ivy crosses her arms. "The way they talk about it, it seems so ugly and crowded there all the time."

"It's not," I say. "Where I live, you can see Central Park. It's like a giant sea of green!" I look at Ivy, expecting her to be making a face, but she's not making a face this time. "Sometimes I go up on the roof of our building and hang out. You can see the Hudson, and sometimes the park. It's really green. You would like it. It's a lot of fun." As I say this, I realize it's been a while since I've spent time in the park. I used to go there every day after school, and sometimes on the weekends with my dad. He would come home early from work just so we could go sledding in the first snow. For so long now, I'd just been rushing home every day to play Earthforge. "Hey, maybe you could visit me in the city sometime?" She stays quiet, then sighs.

Ivy looks around. "I bet *this* place used to be pretty fun." She examines the camp. "I mean, I love it now. There's always a new thing to find, and everything is alive and super creepy. We should come out here at night sometime. This place *is* totally haunted. Maybe we could find Miriam and her animals."

"No way!" I say. "The last thing I need is a bunch of ghosts in my life." I start to imagine the camp at dusk. The dark places even darker. What worlds come alive at night here? I think of the lost girl, and I imagine ghosts and other things creeping through broken floorboards, floating through the meadow to the rec hall.

"Hey!" Ivy shouts, smiling. Then, jumping to her feet, she pushes me, hard, into the water. Laughing, she jumps in after me. Even though it's a little scary, it's nice to not have a chance to overthink things and to get anxious about how I look in a swimsuit, or what might be in the water, or anything else. She makes me laugh. We swim and eat granola bars, and everything has more color than I've seen in a long time.

25

Even though I'm already tired from swimming all morning, it feels good to stay in some kind of routine and go to Krav Maga. Today we work on kicks. Short, fast, front kicks that strike without warning. "This," Nate says, "is for when you are in a tough situation, and there is no getting away or peaceful solution, and you know you gotta do what you gotta do. Krav Maga is about using our natural reactions and being ready to change into a different mode quickly. To recognize the danger and adapt." We lift our legs over and over again until my hips feel so sore I can barely lift them. *If my dad could see me now*, I think. Eli works out in the corner, kicking and punching, his fists making loud *pops* against the bag. Now that I know some of his story, he looks different. Like there's a whole new world inside him that I never would have thought was there. After practice I walk up to him. I feel nervous, but then I think about his little brother. That must be so hard. No wonder he got quiet when I gave him the fishing lure.

"Hey, Eli, how's punching going?" He punches harder—a hollow *thump* on the bag. "Hey, so if you ever want to train or something, maybe we could?" Nothing. He punches left-right combos over and over. I see his fishing rod leaning up against the wall near the bag. I never noticed how intricately carved the wood handle is, and I wonder who made it. "I've never seen a fishing rod like this before." I lift it from its leaning.

"Put it back." His voice vibrates through me. I fumble with the fishing rod, almost letting it hit the floor. "Hey!" he yells. "Be careful, Jesse!" Silence fills the room.

"I'm sorry, I just . . ." but I stop myself. He looks at me, and then, almost out of nowhere, he just nods. I want to say more, but I think I've made it awkward enough. I know he didn't mean to call me Jesse, and I don't think there's anything I can say to smooth things over. I just nod back.

I step out into the fresh air and decide to wait for Aunt Ruthie in the park, which ends up being one of the worst mistakes I've ever made.

26

The park spreads out wide beneath giant spruce trees. In the center is a baseball diamond, where most of the people are. Of course Boon is there, and a bunch of the other kids. I look for Ivy, but I don't see her.

I like to imagine myself playing baseball sometimes. I used to play with my dad, but it got harder when I couldn't hit his faster pitches. We both would get frustrated, and it wasn't as fun anymore. Maybe one day I can try it again.

I sit down beneath one of the trees and watch the kids hit. Usually, no matter where I am, I feel a breeze, a slight wind always coming from the Gray—like I left a window cracked open and the fog could roll in at any time. Sometimes it feels like a cool breeze on a hot day. But right now it smells like someone's basement, stale and far away. Still, my body feels relaxed from all the swimming and Krav Maga. I touch the grass with my fingertips and check my phone. There's a bar of service, so I text my mom about my day and ask if my dad would text me. I see the three dots of her responding, but nothing comes back.

From the field, I hear someone say my name. When I look up, a group of kids is coming around the backstop. Boon's in the front. The blond girl with mirrored sunglasses walks right up to me. "Hi, Sasha. You gonna get sick again today?"

I look down at my feet.

"C'mon, Ally." Boon steps forward, his voice syrupy. "Leave him alone." Boon kneels down in front of me in a catcher's position. He takes a sip from a big cup full of some frozen red drink. "You know I told you it wasn't over, Sashy. I think the best way to make up for you getting sick on me is to even things out a little bit." He takes a long slurp from his cup and then slowly dumps the rest of it onto my NATE'S GYM shirt and my gym bag, turning the green grass red.

"Yeah, it's not as bad as puke, but it works."

The kids behind him look surprised, maybe impressed? I feel frozen, weak, and exhausted. All that training, the weird outburst from Eli earlier, and now this? How do I keep finding myself in these situations? I thought everything was supposed to be simpler here? If I could walk into the Gray at this moment and disappear, I would.

I jump up to wipe the slushie off me, and the crowd steps back. I don't mean anything by it, but the other kids seem to think I'm getting ready to fight. Boon puts his hands up. I try to breathe, to stay present, but my heart is already beating twice as fast and the basement smell is growing stronger. I know what's coming.

"Okay," Boon says, smiling, his hands curling into fists. "I was trying to take it easy on you, but if that's what you want . . ."

Nate talked about being able to adapt fast. I've only been practicing martial arts for a few days, but maybe I *can* stand up for myself. Except I remember how bad it felt when I hurt someone. I don't want that to ever happen again. The moment stretches wide and I think about Jeremy and how scared I felt when all those kids were pressing in on me. I couldn't breathe then, and it's equally as hard to breathe now. I feel the cold red liquid sliding off me. I wish Aunt Ruthie would show up and take me away from all this.

I hear my father's voice. *Toughen up.* I put my hands up because even if I won't fight, I can at least try to keep myself from getting pummeled. Boon's coming closer now. His thin, muscled arms flexing, his fists curled up into baseball-size hammers. He swings, and somehow I manage to duck out of the way. I hear Nate's voice, *In Krav Maga, we always counterpunch.* But I don't. I hold back.

This seems to make Boon even angrier. He turns, almost growling.

"You're dead meat," he says, then lunges at me. Before I know it, his fist lands on my cheek. I fall, expecting everything to turn gray, but it doesn't. I try to get up, but I feel his foot on my lower back, my face sideways in the grass. *How can a day be so great and so terrible at the same time?* Just this morning I was swimming, calm, and now . . . I feel his foot pushing down. I imagine that this is my new reality. Walking to town, Boon and his group constantly harassing me, knocking me into the dirt. Me, unable to fight back because they are too big and there are too many of them. How can I survive the rest of the month like this? My heart beats even faster. I feel the breath going out of me.

"Get up," Boon demands, knowing that I can't.

The crowd of kids chatters around me.

I can't just lie here with my face to the ground. I have to try something.

"Boon. Why are you even doing this?" I grunt into the grass, hoping he'll hear me. He takes his foot off my back, and I gasp. He squats down next to me so I can see his face.

"You started this," he says. I try to think of how to explain it all to him—that I get nervous, and scared, and when that happens I get sick, but it's too much all at once.

A different voice—lower, angrier—disrupts my thoughts.

"Get away from him, Boon." I turn my head in the direction of the voice. Eli is standing above Boon. Boon gets up and so do I, backing away slowly.

"Whatever, Eli. This isn't about you," Boon says.

"I don't care. Take it out on someone else," Eli says.

Boon wipes his mouth and looks around at the crowd, who seems to be waiting to see what happens next. He sticks a finger out at Eli. "This isn't over," he mutters. Then he walks toward the backstop and everyone else falls away.

27

Eli puts out a hand to help me up.

"Thanks." I cough. He nods. Then he turns back toward the street and starts walking away.

"Wait!" I shout. He doesn't stop—he just keeps walking his giant steps. I pick up my stuff and run after him.

"Eli, wait!" I shout again. "Why did you help me?" He stops and turns his head.

"You found Jesse's fishing lure. I guess I owed you one." He smiles a little and keeps walking. He's almost to the sidewalk at the edge of the park when it hits me. Eli and I could become friends—or at least spend time together. If we hung out, I wouldn't have to worry about Boon anymore. I run to catch up with him, then jump out in front of him with my hands out. My voice sounds funny, extra nasally from the punch and a little numb.

"Eli, I need help, and maybe I can help you, too. I know that you walk from the camp to here every day and then back to the ranch to work. Maybe I can walk with you? Maybe I can help you at the ranch? Maybe, maybe you can be . . . my bodyguard?"

Eli looks at me like he might run me over.

"I can pay you! I have some of my bar mitzvah money. Also—maybe you can help me train?" I throw some ridiculous punches and kicks into the air, trying to show him what I mean.

He stares at me. "Nah," he says quietly. Then he turns, but I don't let him go, and for the first time his mouth turns down just a bit.

"Please, Eli. I have to be here for the rest of the month, and Boon is not going to leave me alone." Tears sting in the corners of my eyes. I try to hold them back, but my heart starts to race, my shoulders moving up and down.

"Okay," he says.

The word breaks my breath. I look up. "You, you will?" He's looking at me—the corner of his mouth turned up slightly in an almost-smile. Then he reaches out one of his long arms and puts his big hand on my shoulder.

"But you have to do what I say."

I nod.

"You can't be late. You train how I say. You work hard at the ranch. Oh, and stop talking so much."

I nod. He turns away, but looks back with the slightest grin.

"Wait." Eli says, "How much money are we talking about?"

28

Eli agrees to a simple plan: to walk by Aunt Ruthie's house after he goes fishing in the mornings (when he's on his way to town), and then after class and whatever else, to walk me back as far as the horse ranch, where I will help him with the horses before heading home on my own.

"What about fishing at the old camp dock in the mornings? I could go there with you?" He barely looks at me.

"No."

"I get it," I say. "We all need alone time." I say it the exact same way my mom says it to me—a big emphasis on the word *alone*. When I look up, Eli is staring at me.

"You're a weird kid," he says with no emotion at all.

I nod.

29

The next morning, I text my mom, even though I don't know when she'll read it, to tell her that I made another friend. I also ask her to call me. I think about my dad and wonder if all the changes I've made so far would mean something to him. Am I changing in the right ways? I really wish I could talk to him.

● ● ● ● ● ●

I smell something delicious coming from the kitchen. I don't feel like eating, but I promised Aunt Ruthie I'd always start with breakfast, so I float downstairs to find the table all set. Pancakes stacked high. But Aunt Ruthie is by the door, putting on her coat.

"Aunt Ruthie?" I say, but she doesn't hear me. I feel my stomach turn. Something feels wrong.

"Aunt Ruthie," I say again, this time louder. She looks back at me.

"Good morning, Sasha. There's pancakes and syrup for

you. I'm just taking a morning walk down to the pond. I'll be back in a little while." Then, like she can see the inside of my brain, "Unless, you want to take a walk with me?" I look at the pancakes and decide I don't really feel like being alone right now. I check the clock to make sure I have time to make it back by ten so I can start the walk to town with Eli when he gets here. I scoop up two pancakes and follow her out the door.

We stroll along the small path through the trees. Aunt Ruthie twirls her cane like she's chopping up battle droids. Sometimes it seems like she doesn't want to move at all, like she's out of gas. Today she's full of energy—and something else, something I don't quite recognize.

"You're like Yoda," I say. "You act like you need your cane but . . ." She's already walking on.

Up the side of the hill, where the forest meets the meadow, I see a dark shadow in the trees. It's a cow—no, a bull. It's Lucky. He stands there, his hooves planted, just watching us. He's far away, but it still sends a chill up my spine.

It's early enough when we reach the pond that the frogs are still everywhere. They start to disappear when they hear us, plopping into the water like heavy raindrops. "I like starting my day here when I can," Aunt Ruthie says. "It helps me feel close to Uncle Lou. What about you? What made you want to walk with me so early in the morning?"

"I don't know. I guess I didn't feel like staying in the house. I miss texting my friends, and my parents."

"You know," she says, "your parents want what's best for you. I know it's hard for them to be away from you, too."

"Even my dad?" I say.

"Especially your father. I know how much he loves you."

"He really wants me to change. I don't know if I can." She loops her arm through mine.

Aunt Ruthie walks us to a spot directly across the pond from the Stone of Power. We sit down in the dirt. The frogs slowly peek out of the water, looking directly at us. They either have a message for me or they're about to attack. Then, just above the waterline, I see something I've never noticed before—a tiny trickle of water cascading down the Stone of Power. It looks like the water is coming right through it.

"Aunt Ruthie," I say, pointing. "Do you see that?" She looks at it, deep in thought.

"Oh yes," she says quietly. I recognize her tone. She's getting ready to tell me a story about magic or some ancient secret. I don't know if I feel like hearing it all right now, but Aunt Ruthie is transfixed, the words bubbling from her like the water from the Stone.

"It's getting bolder." We can see more now, a tiny spring of water dripping its way along the Stone's face.

"Remember the story from the Talmud that your uncle Lou used to tell about Akiva?" she begins. "You might not.

That man could tell ten stories all at the same time. But this was one of this favorites that he used to tell all the campers."

"No," I say. "I remember that those stories mattered so much to Uncle Lou, but sometimes it's easier for me to remember his voice than the actual words."

Aunt Ruthie looks straight at me. She has tears in her eyes, but she doesn't look sad.

"I'm so glad you remember his voice, Sasha. When things were getting harder for him, he also liked to come here and look at the Stone. He knew *I* didn't see all the magic or the hidden things that he did, but I loved hearing his stories." She stares into the water, lost in thought and memories. I give her a minute, and she starts again. "Do you remember *why* he loved that story?"

"Something about water and stone together?" I say.

"Yes, about how the water changes the stone." She points right at me. "Your story is all about change, Sasha, like Akiva. When he saw that a trickle of water could change something as solid and stubborn as a stone, he knew he could change and do better, too. If you were to blast a stone like this with a firehose in an attempt to change it, it would be in vain. The only change would be that the stone is wet. It's the slow change, the trickle of water, that matters most. We can't always see it, but little by little, that water is slowly changing the surface of the impossible stone."

She takes my hand and squeezes it. I don't know what to

say. I think I understand her. I don't know if I am patient enough for this. I don't know if my parents are, either. But slow change is still change.

"We better get back," I say. "I don't want to miss Eli." Aunt Ruthie takes a long time getting up. Eventually I help her. She seems tired, like she used all her energy on the way here. She tells me to go on ahead. I make it just in time to catch Eli.

30

Eli walks fast. I try to keep up, but it's like he takes extra-long steps with his already-long legs.

I ask him questions whenever I can catch my breath. "How long have you been taking Krav Maga? What's your favorite school subject?" He ignores me.

"I like coding. Me and Daniel, that's my friend back home, we're trying to learn Python, but it's hard for us. We have some plans to build a game like Earthforge, only there will be a player versus player mode. Do you play any video games?"

"You don't stop until you get answers?" Eli says.

"I like to ask questions. Sorry." Eli stops and looks at me.

"Why didn't you fight back the other day? I mean, even a little?"

I think about how much I want to say, how I feel like I could let everything out about Jeremy and the math book and everything else if I let it, but I can see that any second Eli's going to start walking again. So I keep it simple.

"I didn't want to hurt him. Last time I got upset I hurt someone pretty bad." I feel my fists clench. Eli looks at me with no emotion. Then he nods, turns around, and continues walking.

We take shortcuts to town that I've never seen before, past the outer fence of the horse ranch where Eli works every afternoon. When we get to the end of the fence, before we start down a long meadow that will take us to town, he climbs up on top of the lowest fence plank and puts his hand out. A tall horse with a wild mane and silvery-gray coat whinnies low, trotting over to us. A shiver like a tiny bolt of lightning goes up my spine. It's the horse I saw the first day we came. The one they call the Gray. Eli rests a gentle hand on the horse's muzzle, then takes an apple from his backpack and places it in his flat palm. The horse slowly sniffs the air, and all at once gobbles up the apple with giant teeth.

"That's a cool horse," I say. "What's his name?" Eli doesn't say anything for a while. Finally, he turns his head slowly without actually looking at me.

"He is a she. She's got another name, but everyone just calls her the Gray." His voice is suddenly softer, different, like a kid just being himself. I feel a lump in my throat. I'm thinking now about *my* Gray, but that's not something I want to talk about. Eli says something to her quietly, strokes her neck, then hops off the fence and we continue down the path. When I look back, the Gray is galloping to the far side of the pasture.

31

We come into town by way of a shortcut, and from this direction everything looks a little different—like something out of a storybook. The town is so small that the whole place could fit inside three New York City blocks. There are just a few main streets with a park at the center. Farthest from us is the historical block—where lots of people stop to see the town hall and the old museum. There's also the Hillbertsville Diner and the old candy shop. I think that's where Aunt Ruthie gets her lemon drops. She likes to have them around the house for her dance students.

My phone buzzes in my pocket. It's been a while since I've received texts or calls, so the vibration surprises me. It's a text from my mom. *Glad to hear about your friend. Take it slowly. We love you. Your dad says hello and not to worry about anything. Please try to call us tonight.* When I look up, I notice that Eli is already across the street. Then I think about Boon. He could be anywhere around here. I run to catch up with Eli.

Call her tonight. I think about how much I have to tell

her, about the horse called the Gray, and Ivy, and Aunt Ruthie's cooking. The good things are quickly drowned out by the bad, though. How mad she might get about Krav Maga, or about Boon. Why did *any* of this have to happen at all? Why did the Gray, my Gray, have to come here with me? Why couldn't I have just left it behind in New York City? What if I hadn't thrown up on Boon? I might have had a whole different story to tell her. Maybe he would have been my friend, and I wouldn't have to have a bodyguard.

● ● ● ● ● ●

We get to the gym, but just before we go in, Eli stops and looks at me.

"When will you pay me?"

"I can pay you now?" I unzip my backpack and fish around for my wallet, but he shakes his head.

"Nah, not yet."

"Okay," I say.

We work out hard, practicing kicks and kick defense. I feel bruises developing on my shins. After training, I sit down on one of the benches to rest, but Eli is already by the door. He motions with his head and says, "Time to go. We have lots to do at the ranch today." So, with no break, we walk up the hill, my legs protesting the whole way. I dream about the bus, or the subway, or even a cab. Anything but the pain I'm in. But I keep up. I have no choice. I notice Eli's fishing rod tied to his pack.

"Where did you get your fishing rod?" I ask—and again, nothing. "I see you fishing all the time. Maybe we could go together one morning?"

Eli looks over his shoulder. "Do you ever stop talking?" His voice is loud. "I fish alone."

"Sorry," I say. "Sometimes I get nervous and talk a lot." It gets quiet for a while after that.

"They say the camp is haunted. Do you ever see ghosts?" I ask. I can't help myself.

He stops in his tracks. He turns slowly, and I can feel my heart beating the way it does when my father gets mad at me, like all the air and sound has been sucked away. Eli stares at me, then looks past me and all around, from the hillside to the forest to the sky. His mouth is a straight line.

"I see ghosts all the time," he finally says.

32

We get to the ranch and walk straight into the barn. I can feel the smell in my whole body—dirt, dust, and hay but also leathery saddles and old wood, but most of all, I smell the musky smell of the horses. I don't mind it at all, somehow. The horses lift their heads over the gates of their stalls as we enter. Some show their teeth, neighing and making low sounds like they've been waiting for us to get here. Eli puts his stuff inside a big wooden crate by the barn door. He reaches into another crate and pulls out a bottle labeled GILBERT'S SADDLE SOAP and a few rags. Then he points to the other side of the barn, where saddles rest on stands in a long row.

Eli looks at me. "You get to clean those."

"All of them?" I ask. He doesn't respond. He just walks over to the first saddle. I follow him. He squirts some of the saddle soap on the rag and presses it against the saddle, working in circular motions.

"Just like this, okay? You wanted to help." He shoves the cleaning supplies into my hands. Just about a week and a half ago I was on a trail ride, praying that I would never have to ride a horse again, and now here I am, working in a horse barn. It's hard work, and the horses watch me intently as I scrub the saddles until the soapy rags feel heavy as bricks and I can't lift my arms anymore. After a while, though, the saddles shine and smell like new leather.

I can tell it's getting late, and I know I need to get back. I bring everything back to the crate and put it away before walking over to the first horse stall. A wooden sign carved into the door tells me the horse's name is FLASH. Flash leans his muzzle over the stall and gives me the side-eye. Animals can be scary, but there is something very calm about these horses. I don't know if it is safe to be this close to them, but I know they are good. I stroke Flash's mane.

Down toward the end of the barn, in the last stall, a huge horse is peeking his head out. I recognize him right away—it's Duke! I wonder if he remembers me. "Hi, Duke!" I call out. Duke nods his giant head, or at least it looks that way.

Maybe one day, I think, *I'll ride Duke again*. I promised Aunt Ruthie I would. Thinking of this reminds me that I have to get home.

"I gotta go, Eli," I say. He looks over at me, holding a giant bundle of hay in his arms. The one he calls a palomino in the stall next to him stretches out its long neck to steal a nibble of the hay. Eli points to the trail that winds through the forest, the trail that will take me back to Aunt Ruthie's house.

"Thanks," I say. "See you tomorrow?"

He nods.

I hug the tree line as I walk past the pond and the Stone of Power and back to Aunt Ruthie's. The sun is disappearing behind the trees, and my body aches from the long day. I can't help but think about the Gray, and all the talk of ghosts. The darkening afternoon makes the forest seem different somehow, the light shifting in the shadows of the leaves. I'm used to city streets, doorkeepers, lights, noise, cabs going by. It's so dark here, so quiet, that I feel a little afraid to walk into the woods alone. That's when I hear something behind me. I want to run, and I almost do, but then I hear Eli's voice.

"You have a fishing rod?"

I don't think I've ever heard him say that many words at once. I don't have my own rod, but I'm sure Uncle Lou had one that I can use.

"Yes!" I shout.

"I'll be there at seven." He turns back toward the barn, and I run into the forest, no longer scared—just excited to get home as quickly as I can.

33

Ivy is in the kitchen drinking a big glass of water after her dance lesson. Aunt Ruthie waves her hand over a pan of something hot. "Brownies!" she announces. "These are my special recipe, peanut butter swirl brownies, just for you two." We head out onto the porch to eat our brownies in the twilight evening. Ivy is still sweating from dance practice.

With her mouth so full of brownies that I can barely understand her, she asks, "So, are you okay?" She drinks some water and continues, "I heard about what happened at the baseball field. I wish I could have been there; I would have knocked Boon out myself."

"Yeah," I say nervously. I must smell like horses and hay and probably saddle soap, but Ivy doesn't say anything about it.

"I heard Eli was there? That he stopped him? That must have been a little scary to be in between those two."

I'm not sure what to say, so I don't say anything.

She doesn't push me to answer and instead asks, "Want to go to the camp tomorrow? Maybe we can see the deer again. My mom says that this herd of deer is the same family that's been there since before they built the camp."

"You know a lot about deer," I say.

"They aren't even the oldest in the area, though," she continues. "I guess there are even more ancient families of deer in the hills. Families that have lived for generations! But I've never seen them."

I sit quietly, thinking about Eli, and fishing, and that Ivy might not want to come if she knows he will be there, too. I'm not sure what to think. I don't want to lose Ivy as a friend, but I can't afford to lose Eli, either.

"Well, yeah," I say, my heart beating fast. "But there's just one thing. I'm going fishing . . . with Eli."

She almost spits out her brownie.

"What, are you guys like best friends now?" she says.

"No, I mean, well, he's my bodyguard, and—"

"Bodyguard? What do you mean?"

"I don't know." It suddenly feels embarrassing to say it out loud. "He protects me."

"From Boon?" She looks at me for a while, and I can tell she is planning what to say next. But nothing comes out. Her shoulders relax. She takes another bite of her brownie.

"We're going at seven if you want to come. We could all go together?" I say.

She nods, so I know she hears me. She lets her hair fall dramatically in front of her face.

"Maybe," she says.

• • • • • •

That night, Aunt Ruthie helps me use her landline to call my mom. I usually don't like talking on the phone, but it's great to hear her voice.

I tell her all about the horses, Eli, Ivy, fishing, and exploring the camp. She seems so happy to hear it all. Then she asks, "Have you been taking your medicine? How are you feeling? Are you having difficult dreams? Not too tired, I hope?"

"It's going okay, I guess. I forgot to take it once, and it made my sleep kind of weird . . ." I trail off, wanting to tell her about Krav Maga and how much I like it. But I don't. I don't mention Boon or the Gray or bodyguards or anything like that.

"Is Dad there?" I ask instead.

"He's still at work, but he wants you to know he loves you very much." I take a deep breath. I wish I could hear him tell me himself.

34

That night I have what my mom calls a difficult dream, and it feels so real. My mind and body fight in the half-sleep, half-awake place, like a fish caught on a line. In the dream, I run to the pond. The water, the trees, the sky—they're all different shades of gray. Mist swirls around the trunks of trees. The forest smells like moldy leaves. I listen for the birds, but none are singing. I try to find the frogs, but none are croaking. I hear something far off—a howling. My heart pounds loudly, but then I hear something else, hoofbeats? I walk to the edge of the pond, where the water looks like dark ice. I try to see my face in the water, but it's only a shadow. I hear the noise again, a thump, but nearer now. I look across the pond at the Stone of Power, and it is completely the same. Unchanged. It makes me feel a little better. The water is trickling down the one side. *Thump thump!* I hear the noise again, hard hoofbeats on the ground. Then, I see Eli standing there in his green jacket and heavy boots, his hood pulled tight so I can't really see his face. He holds his fishing rod in one hand and in the other he holds the reins to a horse that stands in the mist far behind him. He's looking straight at me. "Eli!" I call out, but by then I feel the trees closing in around me, spinning. I lose my balance. I'm already falling, slipping on some mud—or something else.

I wake up and find my breath. This isn't the first rough morning I've ever had. Sometimes the Gray finds its way into my dreams. Usually I would grab my phone and look at things on it to help me calm down, but this time I try grounding. 5—Look: Look for five things around you and say them out loud. I feel silly saying it to the air, but I do it anyway.

"Window, pillow, tree, drawing, water cup." 4—Feel: Find four things you can feel and say them out loud. "My foot in a sock, my fingers wiggling in front of my face, my heartbeat, my voice saying things out loud." Three is sounds, but I'm already starting to feel better. I think about fishing, and I start to get excited. I need to go get some worms.

• • • • • •

It's so early that Aunt Ruthie isn't even awake yet. I sneak out the door, grab a bucket, and walk toward the pond to collect worms for bait. The early morning mist is heavy, but the sunlight is already seeping through. The forest is full of familiar sounds, owls hooting and yips from dogs and maybe even a horse whinnying in the distance. I hear the frogs croaking in the pond and the birds singing their morning songs.

I set my bucket down at the edge of the pond and look across at the Stone of Power. For a moment, I imagine Eli there, just like in the dream. The water is chilly, but I reach into the cold, muddy bank and pull up a handful of dirt and clay, just like I used to do with Uncle Lou. I flip it over and watch the worms wriggling through the dark mud. I grab a few more handfuls and shove them into the bucket. *Perfect.* When I get back to the house, Aunt Ruthie is waiting on the porch. "I was worried," she says. "It's so early in the morning." Then she suddenly puts her hands on the porch railing. She looks like she might fall down. I run over to catch her.

"I'm fine," she says. "I just get a little dizzy sometimes."

In the kitchen, she puts the tea kettle on the stove. "I'm sorry," I say. "I got excited about fishing, so I got up early and went to the pond to get some worms. I should have told you first." She nods and takes sips of tea.

"I heard noises from your room—that's what woke me up. Did you have a nightmare?"

I don't answer right away.

"Not exactly a nightmare, but a weird dream, yes. I was at the pond, but I was in the Gray." She nods. "Everything was quiet, and then I saw Eli there, and I even saw a horse! When I woke up, I tried grounding, and it helped."

"I'm so happy to hear this," she says. "There's something enchanting about dreams. That place between sleep and wakefulness. Like our mind is strong but also vulnerable at the same time. Your uncle Lou used to have the strangest nightmares, and the most wonderful dreams just before waking up. Worlds within worlds, he would say."

"I'm sorry, Aunt Ruthie. I promise to let you know what I'm doing."

"I'm fine. Fine. Just remember to pay attention to the day. Sometimes there are reasons our minds take us places we don't expect." Then she smiles like she didn't just say something that sounded like the moral of a story. "Let's keep talking over breakfast. It's way too early to not be drinking tea."

35

Aunt Ruthie makes a huge frosty mug of chocolate milk for me, and oatmeal with cinnamon. She sprinkles marshmallows into both. I take out my phone, hoping to see a text from Daniel. There isn't one, but there is one from Mom. *Loved talking to you last night.* Then there's a bunch of emojis. I read a few more texts from my mom. *Life is boring here without you. Miss you. Love you.* I text back *love you too*, not knowing when it might reach her. My phone still has dirt in the corners from when I left it at the camp. I don't think I've ever let it get this dirty before. I start to clean it and accidently swipe my Discord app. It doesn't open, but it makes me think about video games, feel a surge of energy running through my arms. For a moment I forget about everything and imagine myself settling into my big chair in my room and playing Earthforge all day. "Aunt Ruthie, you really need to get Wi-Fi." She sips her tea.

"I do *not* need weefee. I do *not* need to be staring at some little box all day. You don't see Luke Skywalker staring at his phone all day." She takes one last sip before getting up. Moments later, she calls me out to the front porch. She hands me an old fishing rod and helps me practice casting. She talks about the rod and how it needs all kinds of new things, but I don't really know enough about fishing to recognize the words. She tries to give me an old cap, one of Uncle Lou's hats that has vibrant, multicolored fishing lures stuck all over it, but I don't take it because it seems like all those hooks will get stuck in my head. I grab a backpack loaded up with everything I need.

By 6:57, Eli is standing on the gravel road waiting for me. We walk silently in the cold morning for a long time, but at least he walks slowly enough that I can keep up. Finally, I hold up the bucket. "I got us some worms." He nods but doesn't look. I try to hold it back, but then I say, "I got them from the pond super early this morning. I actually thought I saw you there in a dream." I immediately wish I hadn't said it. Eli stops, and for a moment he seems like a different kid. But it passes quickly. He looks down at the bucket.

"Those look like good ones," he mutters in his low voice.

Now that he's talked, though, all my questions fly out.

"So, what kind of fish do you catch? Do you eat them? I went fishing once with my dad in Montauk. My friend Daniel caught a fluke on his first cast, so I spent the whole day trying to catch one, too. I finally did, but I had to throw it back. I don't know if . . ."

"Bass, sometimes walleyes, maybe a catfish." He pulls

a granola bar out of his pocket and takes a bite. The abandoned camp is so quiet in the early morning.

"Did you ever go here? To the camp?" I ask.

"One summer I did. I was younger than Jess—" He stops.

"I wonder why someone doesn't open up a new camp," I say.

We walk past the old bunks. Butterflies fill the path, fluttering in every direction—bright blue-and-white streaks, like the wind is coming to life. Just ahead in the meadow, the deer graze in the long grass that used to be a baseball field. Ivy would want to see this. I look around to see if she's already at the dock, but no one is there.

Eli sets everything up, and I try to do what he does, but I think he can tell I haven't fished in a while. He pulls out a cottage cheese container.

"Is that your breakfast?" I ask.

He looks at me, half smiling.

"Yeah." He opens the lid. Inside something dark is wriggling around the sides of the container. "These are night crawlers. Just like your worms, only bigger. They're delicious." He grabs one by the end and holds it up to my face. It's the size of my pinky. "Try it."

I don't know what to do. Does he mean it? I put my hand out cautiously, but by then he is laughing. Then, in one fast move, he folds the worm in half and, with a squish, sticks it onto a hook. He leans back and lightly casts his line out into the water, the bobber plopping onto the glassy surface.

I tie some sinkers onto my line and then the hook. I reach into the cottage cheese container and find a big worm. I try to put it onto the hook, but the worm is so strong, every time I try to stick it on the hook it slides off. I finally get it, press down, and feel a sharp sting. "Ouch!"

"What happened?" Eli looks over. A small spot of blood spills out from where the hook punctured my finger. "Man, you scared all the fish for that?"

"Ha, yeah," I fake laugh. And that's when I notice it. My fishing rod has wood carvings in the handle just like Eli's. Mine are worn, though—smoother than his. "I think my uncle carved your fishing rod." Eli looks to my fishing rod, then back at his. Then he nods and grabs the worm container.

"Let me help you." He shows me how to put the worm on and how to cast, and then we're fishing. Our lines float in the water as the sun slowly rises into the quiet sky. The deer are still grazing in the meadow. That's when I see Ivy.

She rides her bike down to the edge of the meadow. She gets off her bike, points to the deer, and puts her hands out like she can't believe it. I mouth *I know* in her direction. Eventually she walks her bike across the meadow, moving as quietly as she can. Eli doesn't look at her.

"Did you see the stag?" Her voice is shaky.

I nod. We watch the deer for a little bit.

"So," she says. "How's fishing?"

"It's quiet," I say.

Ivy looks over at Eli, and then crosses her arms.

"Hi, Eli." He glances at her then looks back to the water.

I hold up my fishing rod. "Want to give it a try? I just gave it my first okay cast." But she's staring at Eli's hair, and when I look, I see that there's some fishing line and a tiny sinker tangled in the ends of his curls. Ivy starts laughing, and she can't stop. Her laughter makes me start to laugh, too. Pretty soon we are both laughing so hard we can barely stand up.

"What?" Eli turns to us, his hands balled into fists. "What is it?" He sees us looking at his hair, so he feels the sides of it, finds the tangle, and pulls it out. "What? You think this is funny?" He throws it onto the dock, but then something else happens. I feel a heavy tug on my line, a big one. The rod almost jerks out of my grip. I grab it tight with both hands, but it pulls me to the edge of the dock. Eli puts his rod down. "C'mon," he says. "Reel it in."

Ivy grabs a net from the dock. I try to reel it in, but it's hard. "Pull up on it," Eli says, and I do. I wind and wind, the fish getting closer and closer until its spiky fin streams through the water. Eli grabs my rod, too. Together we pull up one last time. The fish launches high in the air then straight down, slapping into Eli and me. We fall back, the fish frantically flopping around the dock. Ivy tries to net it, but eventually Eli gets it and wrestles it under his arm so he can take the hook out and dump it into the bucket.

After he gets the fish in there, we all sit on the wet dock, breathing heavily, our hands fishy and wormy and our faces soaked. Ivy holds up the net. "Well, I did nothing."

Eli smiles, and then his face breaks into laughter like I've never seen, like turning on a light in the darkest room, and we all laugh until our stomachs hurt.

Ivy takes pictures of the fish in the bucket, and we eat peanut butter chocolate brownies before we have to get going.

"Once," Eli says while packing up his gear, "I saw a giant catfish swim beneath the dock. It was huge—it had to be bigger than me."

"Oh," Ivy says. "You mean the Camp Akiva lake monster?"

"I don't know, but it was huge. It was definitely a monster."

Ivy gets on her bike. "I have to hurry up to my piano lessons. Can't wait to fish again!" she shouts before riding off through the meadow and up the hill.

We move fast through the meadow, realizing that we are cutting it close for making it to the gym in time for class. We take shortcuts and, for my sake, are careful to avoid poison ivy and all the other things that live in the abandoned places of the old camp. We stop at the horse ranch so Eli can put our fish in the old fridge in the barn, and then we jog almost the entire way to the gym. I stop to rest a few times, and Eli waits silently for me. I can tell he's annoyed. I'm not a good runner. When I was little, I got second place in a cross-country meet with hundreds of schools. I thought running would be my thing, but everyone grew up and got faster than me. My dad tried to get me to run with him through Central Park every day, but I never did. That was when he started saying "Don't be a quitter" and telling me that I needed to toughen up. At least the first time I can remember.

Running is getting a little better now. My legs hurt, but they feel stronger. But it's not just running that's getting better. Nate tells me that he sees me improving. This is something I am *not* used to. Usually, I am stuck between my mom, who thinks everything I do is perfect and special, and my dad, where it's never enough. Once, our rabbi told me my singing was *improving*. I'm still not sure if he was telling the truth, but I liked what he said. To me it felt like a good place to be: not perfect but headed in the direction of getting better.

36

After class, we decide to take a different way back. We turn the corner onto the main street in town. It's the busiest I've ever seen it. The Hillbertsville Diner is full of people eating outside and inside. There's a banner in a big arch over the street with a picture of a Ferris wheel that says SUMMER FESTIVAL JULY 4! I'd usually be in the city for July Fourth. When I first got here, all I could think about was getting home, but now I'm not sure. I think I'm starting to like it here. We pass by the old candy shop. There's a giant sign in the window that reads FRESH FUDGE. I think about Aunt Ruthie. Maybe getting her some fudge would be a nice way of saying sorry for worrying her this morning.

"I'm gonna get some before we go back," I say, pointing to the sign. Eli shakes his head.

"None for me. I'll wait out here."

Inside the store, there are rows of different kinds of candy and a huge case full of cookies and ice cream. There's even a long counter with high stools like in some old movie. I see Boon and Ally, who is wearing her sunglasses, even inside, and a few other boys sitting at the counter with giant milkshakes. They don't see me yet. I look back at the window, but Eli is nowhere in sight.

I know that Nate always teaches us that the best self-defense is *not* being where the danger is. I think about this. What do I *want* to do? Should I run? I want to get the fudge for Aunt Ruthie. I want to be able to feel safe. I want to maybe have some control over what happens to me. I hear laughter coming from Boon and his friends, but they aren't laughing at me—they are pointing at a young girl maybe half their age with her hair tied into pigtails around a face bursting with freckles. She's holding an empty cone. All the ice cream, it seems, has fallen onto her shirt in a giant white blob. Ally makes fake crying faces at her. I want to help her. I know what it's like to be her. But I'm not sure what to do. That's when Boon sees me.

"Well, look who it is," he says. But all I see is the little girl wiping her shirt, trying not to cry. I take a deep breath—in through the nose, out through the mouth.

"Why can't you leave her alone?" I say. It feels like time stops. The little girl stares at me, astonished. Her friends stand up and group around her. Behind the counter, a man with a giant handlebar mustache and apron walks up to us. His voice breaks the silence.

"All right, let's calm down. Can I get everyone—"

But it's too late. Boon jumps up, his stool crashing to the floor. I back up toward the door as they all get up. What have I done? I turn and run through aisles of candy and stuffed animals, out onto the sidewalk.

They burst out of the door after me: Boon, Ally, two others I've heard him call Johnny and Oscar, and a few other kids I haven't seen before. Then the door opens wider and the little girl with freckles comes out, too, followed by her friends, all holding ice cream cones. People on the street start to gather around, wanting to see what the commotion is about. I look for Eli.

"So, why don't you go back to the city and mind your own business?" Johnny says as he and Oscar step forward, followed by Boon, their fists balled up. I step back and trip over a bump in the sidewalk. I almost fall, but catch myself just in time to stand up straight. Boon and his friends come forward a little more. That's when Eli steps out from a doorway and stands, gigantic, right behind me, his arms crossed. Boon and his friends stop, their feet slipping, bumping into each other.

"Boon," I say, crossing my arms, too. "I'd like you to meet my bodyguard. Anything you want to say to me, you can say to him." Boon steps back and turns to the others.

"C'mon, we don't have to be afraid," he says to them. But they're all looking down. "C'mon, Johnny, you can't bail on me. Oscar?" But one by one they shake their heads and turn away, getting on their bikes and riding off until only Boon and Ally are left.

"We used to be friends, Eli," Boon says, his body trembling. I look up at Eli, who is unmoving, just staring at Boon. He shakes his head. Then, out of the crowd, the little girl steps forward, the ice cream on her shirt completely melted now. She walks up to Boon and points her finger in his face.

"Hahaha!" she shouts, and then laughter grows among the crowd until I can't tell if it's real laughter or if they're making fun of him. It gets louder and louder until Boon and Ally jump on their bikes and escape.

I almost feel bad for him.

Boon looks back at us, his face twisted in rage, while the crowd watches him go, and I stand with my arms crossed like a tough guy. The little girl runs up and sticks out her hand to me, or maybe to Eli, and we high-five. The next thing I know, there are hands everywhere. We are high-fiving and laughing. Even Eli is smiling.

● ● ● ● ● ●

On the way to the ranch, I try to get Eli to talk about how awesome it all was. But he stays quiet, so I stop. I still feel the adrenaline coursing through my body, and I use it keep up with Eli. We wind our way out of town, walking up, up until we can finally see the ranch in the distance. The Gray is galloping end to end in a wide stable, tearing up the meadow, rearing up into the air like she could leap over the fence with ease. Then, beyond that is the forest and the path back to Aunt Ruthie's. I am starting to understand the land, starting to see it like a map in my head. All the walking is comforting, like my body is finally learning a new routine that's about more than just keeping a schedule.

We stop at the barn, and this time Eli asks me to make sure that all the saddles on the racks have the right straps and cinches connected. I go through each one, pulling and tightening. I used to think saddles were just something that clipped on, but they're actually pretty complex. Eli asks me to fill the water barrels for all the horses. It's hard work, but I don't mind. I like being around the horses. I start with Flash. He puts his muzzle under the hose. I do the same for Blackberry, a small dark horse with a white star on his forehead. Blackberry makes bubbles in the water. Just above us is a wide loft where hay is stacked to the ceiling. I remember the story Ivy told me, about what happened here. Because I'm staring, I forget about the water until it starts overflowing the barrel.

"Pay attention," Eli grumbles. "There's nothing to see up there."

"Sorry! Sorry, Blackberry." I sweep the water toward a drain in the floor. It seems to entertain the horses. When I'm done sweeping and filling the rest of the barrels, I check in with Eli, and he tells me to go home. I grab my bag and run out of the barn to make it back in time for dinner.

Aunt Ruthie lets me tell her all about my day. I tell her almost everything. I want to tell her how we stood up to Boon, but what if she tells my parents? What if she gets mad? So I leave it out. Instead I tell her all about Flash, and Blackberry, and making the barrel overflow.

37

I bound down the stairs the next morning, not sure if I've overslept. I hope I haven't missed Eli. I look out the door, and there he is, standing on the gravel road, but he's not alone. Aunt Ruthie is outside on the porch. "Come on inside. I'll make eggs!" she says. "Can't miss breakfast."

Eli takes a side step in the gravel. "It's okay, I'll wait here."

Aunt Ruthie quietly walks up the path to where Eli stands in the road. She looks tiny next to him, small but still in complete control of how she moves. She slips her arm into his. She's telling him something I can't hear. He laughs a little, looks at me, and then, taking her arm, comes down the path. She's like a planet, pulling everyone into her orbit.

We eat eggs cooked with onions that I'm sure we will hate. But they're delicious.

"How are the horses?" Aunt Ruthie asks Eli.

"Good," he says. "Horses are always good."

"And how's your father?" Eli looks up from his eggs.

"Good." We all look at each other. Aunt Ruthie sets down her coffee mug with a loud *clunk*.

"Tell us about your *favorite* horse, Eli." He pushes his eggs around his plate and takes a bite of his toast but doesn't say anything. I can't stand the silence, so I jump in.

"I met that really cool horse the other afternoon. The one with the silvery-gray coat and dark black mane, and she can run super fast. They call her the Gray." Aunt Ruthie looks at me.

"The Gray? Now isn't that interesting? I like that name." And just like she's performed some kind of Jedi mind trick, Eli starts to talk.

"She has another name, but everyone calls her that right now. They think she's too wild. She's fast, but she's not built for racing. They tried to train her for trail rides, but she throws everyone who tries to get on her—except me and Jesse. Jake, the ranch owner, got really mad. He was going to get rid of her, but my little brother, Jesse, really liked her and begged my dad to keep her around. So, he convinced Jake to keep her. We used to ride her all the time after school—all the way to Far Point Meadow. Jesse used to . . ."

Aunt Ruthie puts her hand on top of Eli's.

"That's wonderful," she says. For a moment, Eli looks like a young kid—like the kid he is supposed to be. "Eli, you should take this one riding again one day," she says, pointing to me. "I know you're spending a lot of time *working* with the horses, but you have to get back *on* a horse sometime."

"We'd better get going if we're going to make it on time," I say, trying to change the subject.

"Just a moment," Aunt Ruthie says, walking us to the door. She reaches down and picks up Eli's fishing rod. I try to warn her not to touch it, but she already has it in her hands. "This is one of Lou's? My husband. He made this."

"My mom gave it to me," Eli whispers. She hands it back and nods. Then Aunt Ruthie gives us brown paper bags filled with snacks, which are completely gone by the time we leave the road to head into the forest.

38

Today is very different from yesterday. The fish aren't biting, and there aren't any deer. Frustrated, we leave early. At least the forest is alive with birdsong, and the sunlight is starting to push through the leaves. It's getting warmer. A million bugs jet across the surface of the pond. Frogs croak so loud that I can feel the vibrations in my chest. At first, the croaks are separate, but the closer we get, the more they become one rhythm, until it sounds like one giant frog.

"Do you hear that?" I say. "Maybe there is a giant frog living under the Stone of Power."

"The what?" Eli says.

I realize that I've never referred to it by name with anyone other than Aunt Ruthie and Uncle Lou.

"Oh, that's just what my uncle Lou called it: the Stone of Power. I still call it that sometimes. It reminds me of him."

"Cool," Eli says. "Let's go check it out." We walk around the pond to the mossy, cushioned hill on top of the stone. Then we lean over and look down. I find the trickle of water running down over the Stone's surface and put my finger into the stream, letting it drip over my finger. "Do you know the story of Akiva and the stone?"

"Akiva? Like the camp?" Eli says.

"Yeah," I say.

"Do you ever wonder what's under this thing?" Eli says before I can say anything else. He knocks on the Stone like it's a door. I hear his knuckles scrape against the hard rock.

"Under it?" I ask.

"Yeah, I mean, you'd have to get into that water and dive down." He picks up a pebble and drops it into the murky water. It disappears immediately, like it fell into mushroom soup.

"I don't think I could get into *that* water," I say.

"Yeah, some ponds are for swimming, but this is not one of them. I know another place with a stone a lot like this one."

"Another one? Like this?" But Eli stays silent.

We stare at the water for a while. I lay my hand flat on the Stone like it's some holy thing. Then we continue on our way to town.

39

This time the Gray is at the fence when we pass by. There's a man standing there, too, feeding her something. He's tall with dark, curly hair beneath a baseball cap. He holds a rope in his hand that's attached to a loose-fitting halter.

"Hey, Pop," Eli says. His dad doesn't say anything. Eli walks up and strokes the horse's mane. She throws her head back a little, like she's trying to play. His dad steps back, makes some space.

"Pop, this is Sasha. He's working with me at the ranch for the summer." He looks at me and tips his hat, then he turns back to Eli.

"You ridden her lately?" his dad asks. Eli shakes his head. "She needs to be ridden sometimes, you know, kid." His words sound like they weigh thousands of pounds. Eli takes his backpack off and leans his fishing rod against it. He looks back at me, then climbs up on the fence. "Easy now, girl," his dad says in a low voice. "Easy now." He hands Eli the rope and, for a moment, it looks like Eli might just jump over the fence and ride bareback into the meadow like he's done that a thousand times before. But when he gets to the top of the fence, he stops, looking around like he sees something, then just jumps down and hands the rope back to his father.

"We got to get to town, Pop. I'll be back for work."

We head to town, the Gray neighing wildly behind us as we go. Before long, we see the town up ahead. If we keep walking fast, we'll make it to Nate's Gym just in time. I hate being late for anything.

"You didn't want to ride her?" I finally ask. He doesn't say anything, just swings his arms, his hands brushing up against the long weeds on the trail and sending billowy fluff into the air. "I mean, she seemed like she wanted you to?"

He stops and looks at me. "You know what? I remember that day you and your aunt came out to ride. Have you even been back on a horse since Duke threw you off? You know you're supposed to get right back on a horse if it throws you? Obviously, it's not that easy."

I've heard this so many times I can feel it in my bones. I'm frustrated. We are maybe becoming friends, finally talking to each other. I shouldn't say anything, but I can't stop myself. "I know all about getting back on. I know it's what I'm supposed to do. But if it's so true, why don't you do it?"

He clenches his jaw.

"I can't," he says. "I have my reasons. What's your excuse?"

"I have my reasons, too." I'm not ready to tell him about

my anxiety, or *my* Gray. That would ruin everything. We stand there awkwardly, time pressing down on us until finally he just looks away and starts walking again.

We spend the afternoon practicing defenses against chokes and doing push-ups and a bunch of other things that make my whole body hurt. By the time we're walking back to the ranch, I am beyond sore. Eli still isn't really talking to me except to tell me the work that needs to be done.

Flash and Blackberry nod their heads as we walk into the barn. I stroke their manes and give each of them an apple from the big barrel, and then we get to work. I bring in blankets from outside the barn and stack them near the saddles for the next day's trail rides. Flash is leaning his long neck as far as he can out of his stall, like he's trying to bend all the way to the ground. That's when I see his half-eaten apple lying on the ground just out of his reach. By now, most of the horses have noticed the apple, too. I look around, then walk over to the apple, pick it up, and hold it out to Flash. He devours it. The other horses start bobbing their heads up and down, whinnying like a dozen kids screaming, "It's not fair!" I try to find Eli, but I don't see him anywhere. I stare at the barrel of juicy red apples. I don't want Eli to get mad at me, but I can't help it. I fill my arms with apples, feeding one to each horse. They chomp on the apples, spitting pieces onto the hay. They are happy. So happy.

"So?" comes a voice from behind me. "I leave for a few minutes and you're giving out apples to all the horses?"

"But they love them," I say, my voice trembling.

Eli looks around, and for a moment it looks like he actually smiles. "You better get going."

I get my stuff together and head for the door.

"Just remember," Eli says, and I turn around. "Palm up and flat." He holds an apple in his palm—flat as a board. "Unless you *want* to lose your fingers next time?"

He laughs like he's imagining me losing my fingers. I don't laugh. His face changes. "Hey," he says, nicely now. "You're doing a good job." Then he punches my arm lightly.

I pretend to block and counter, and he leans backward like my punch landed hard.

40

When I get home, I see Ivy and Aunt Ruthie through the window, dancing. I sit down on the porch so I don't disturb the lesson. I tap my feet to the quick horns and drumbeats of the music mixed with the low sounds of their voices and look up at the wide sky. Storm clouds swirl high above, threatening rain. A wave of tiredness from the long day rolls over me. I yawn, resting my face in my hands and thinking about everything that has happened. Today I smell like apples, hay, and horses, and I don't mind it at all. My phone suddenly vibrates. I look down, and there's a text from Daniel! There must have been a moment of reception. I forgot I was even carrying my phone.

Sash! I know I'm not supposed to text you. I hope you don't get in trouble. I had to tell you. I got a record in my latest speedrun! Are you alive?

I haven't really been thinking about coding or gaming lately. But at seeing his words, I suddenly feel a keyboard beneath my fingers, a game controller in my hands. I imagine blocks of code spinning in the air all around me, and the feel of all my favorite games. I can see the viewpoint in the games so clearly in my mind—I feel the energy of it in my body. I hear Daniel's voice. I even smell the warm cookies that his mom usually makes us when we work on our games together.

Suddenly I want to be there so badly. My stomach aches, and I fold over a little. The world of video games and coding is small, self-contained. I can make it what I want it to be or just play it again and again until I clear all the levels. I can even find videos online to guide me when I get stuck on a map or in a boss fight. But here the world is so big, so out of control. So unpredictable. I never know what I'll see by the dock, or if I'll catch a fish, or if the deer will be in the meadow. Uncle Lou said that it's okay not to know everything that's going to happen. It's starting to feel like maybe that's true.

I quickly text Daniel back. I'm struggling to think of something to say, so I just type: *I'm alive.* I see the blinking dots that indicate he's responding, and with a *pop*, a happy face and a thumbs-up light up the screen. Then the words slowly materialize: *I hung out with Jeremy the other day.* Jeremy? Hung out with him? I wait for more, but by now all the bars have gone away. "Why?" I yell at my phone. I refresh it, but nothing changes. I start to write back to Daniel anyway. I type: *Jeremy?* That doesn't make sense. Then all at once, my body shudders as I remember that day, the book hitting my friend in the face, the blood on the floor. People shouting. My breath gets shallow. Clouds swirl in the sky. It starts to sprinkle, but before long rain is falling in giant drops. I take some deep breaths and let the rain splash down on me. I think of Flash, so happy eating his apple, and even Duke in his stall, and the thought of the horses calms me down. I focus with all my strength on the dance music coming through the window and the warm orangey-yellow light inside the house. I feel calm.

I'm getting better at this.

41

"You're soaked," Ivy calls from the doorway. It's true. It feels good, though. She pulls me inside. Aunt Ruthie throws a towel at my head.

"You've always loved the rain. When you were tiny—in diapers even—you would just splash down into any mud puddle you could find."

"Aunt Ruthie!" I say, feeling my face flush.

"Don't become a tomato. Listen, you just love the water. I get it. It feels like getting clean."

"I love it, too," Ivy says. "I like it better when it rains. There are more fireflies, and the forest is greener after. Plus, you can sit under a blanket and watch movies or draw or whatever." Ivy slides me a small plate with saltines on it. Aunt Ruthie is pouring ingredients into a giant pot, then she puts a bowl full of cold yellow goop in front of us.

"Okay, help me make the matzo balls. But don't squeeze them too tight, and *do not* roll them too much." She reaches into the bowl and demonstrates, her eyes fixed, rolling the matzo mixture gently and then placing the first ball down on waxed paper. "I got the schmaltz just right!"

"What's schmaltz?" Ivy asks.

"Don't ask," I say as I pull a glob from the bowl and start rolling it. Ivy dips her hand into a bowl of water first then does the same.

"So," she says, "Eli seems kind of . . . normal now? Like not that angry?"

"Yeah," I say. She puts a matzo ball on the waxed paper. It looks terrible, but I don't say anything.

"Did you work at the ranch today?" she asks.

"I gave so many apples to the horses. Too many. At first I thought Eli was mad, but maybe he thought it was funny?" I hold up a matzo ball—mine are twice as big as hers.

"Do you ever worry that he might . . . freak out?"

"No!" I say, my voice suddenly loud. "We don't know everything that happened. You told me stuff you heard, and I know you live here and everything, but I don't, so it feels like maybe I can give him a chance since I don't know the whole story—maybe none of us knows the real story . . . And anyway, it's in the past, isn't it?"

Ivy looks at me, a little stunned, brushing the green part of her hair away from her eyes.

"Maybe he acts like a loner because everyone leaves him alone," I continue. "Who helped him when all that stuff happened, anyway? Maybe if people would talk to him, he might feel better. I mean, it took me one day here, and I almost got beat up. I would have if I didn't throw up all over Boon. Maybe it's not easy to make friends here?"

Silence. I realize that I may have gone too far. Ivy keeps silently rolling her matzo balls.

"You know," Aunt Ruthie says, crossing her arms. She's holding a kitchen knife like a lightsaber, carrot guts sliding off the blade. "I don't know everything that happened in the barn that day, either, and I don't want to wish ill on anyone, but that trainer had something coming for what he did to that family. They went through so much. I wish we'd tried to give them more food when everything happened. We ought to try to see if we can reach out to Eli's dad now. Maybe we can give him some matzo ball soup. This is going to be a good batch—"

She looks down at our tray and then rolls her eyes. "Or not—you've got to be kidding me!" She takes all our matzo balls and puts them into a giant heap, then plops them back into the bowl. "All right, you two. Start over. Small, even, identical spheres!"

Then, without warning, Ivy drops one of her lopsided matzo balls into the water and it splashes everywhere. For a few seconds, everything is silent, then Aunt Ruthie lets out a loud laugh, and we can't help but start laughing, too.

42

Before bed, I look to see if Daniel has texted me back, but he hasn't, so I play a few games of Drop the Block. I used to think that doing this helped me fall asleep. But it just looks so bright, and it makes me *more* awake. I turn it off and set the phone on the nightstand. I remember to take my medicine.

"Good night, Sasha," Aunt Ruthie says, peeking in the doorway. "You okay?"

I look at her. "Yeah," I say without thinking. My mother asks me this all the time. I always wonder how to answer. If I say no, it becomes a long and sometimes confusing conversation. If I say yes, it's shorter, and she usually looks happier. Aunt Ruthie smiles before I can say another word. "Good, because I have some books to read and some music to listen to."

"Aunt Ruthie?"

She opens the door wider.

"Why do you think Ivy is friends with Boon?"

She walks in, sits down on the edge of my bed, and takes

a deep breath. I sense a story coming on. "I don't know, but if I had to guess . . ." She pauses to take a sip of tea. "She doesn't have a lot of choices. Do you know I was the first Jewish person she ever talked to? We all grow up differently. Different speeds, you know? We take some people with us, and we leave some people behind. But it's always hard, no matter what. It's the hardest, though, when things break apart."

I nod, pretending I understand her.

"Ivy and Boon and all those other kids have been in this town for a long time. Some of them have had to deal with some really tough stuff. You know, Rabbi Akiva taught that loving your neighbor was one of the most important principles of the Torah. That's one of the reasons the camp was named after him. I think that's what Uncle Lou and I loved so much about the camp. It brought people together."

"What does Boon have to deal with?" I say. "Nobody messes with him. He's just a big jerk."

She turns toward me. "Sometimes *the world itself* messes with us. You know all about that. When all that stuff happened with Eli and Jesse, it affected Boon, too. He lost one of his best friends. Think about how Obi-Wan felt when he lost Anakin, or had to leave Luke? I don't think that part was anybody's fault. It's what we call collateral damage."

"What?" I say. "I don't think . . ."

"Never mind, but you get what I mean. Boon got hurt,

too, and maybe that's why he acts so mean sometimes. I'm not saying it's right, but sometimes our enemies aren't all evil, even though they might need a good punch in the mouth at times."

I almost miss the last part of what she says because my eyes are suddenly heavy with sleep.

"Good night, Sasha."

43

The next afternoon, it's still drizzling. We duck into the barn and Eli gets ready for work. I wonder what he'll have me do today. I take a long look around. It's huge inside this barn, like a cavern in some forgotten kingdom. Flash, Blackberry, and the other horses lean their huge heads out of their stalls when they hear us come in. They make low sounds when Eli walks past them. There's hay everywhere—on the floor and in huge bales stacked in the loft. Maybe more hay just got delivered. There are dark birds, or some other animal, huddled at the very top of a bale high in the loft. I count the stalls one by one—there are fourteen. Eli grabs a shiny silver shovel, and we walk to the very last stall with a painted board that says DUKE. Just below that, a small sign says HORSE PEOPLE ARE STABLE PEOPLE.

"Duke!" I say. Eli looks back at me while he puts on the biggest gloves I've ever seen and slips on rubber boots over his shoes.

"That's right," he says. "You know Duke. Then you won't mind?" He lifts the shovel, holding it out in front of me. "Put it *all* in the bin." He points toward a big blue bin with a black lid. The shovel is heavy. I go into Duke's stall, which actually opens up to the outside, too, like a little porch. That's where he is, neighing in a rumbly way out in the afternoon drizzle.

"All right, Duke," I say. "I've come for your poop." Duke flips up an ear then turns his head toward me. Before I know it, his giant muzzle is sniffing me.

"Here," Eli says. "Give him this." He throws me an apple, which I don't catch, but Duke is happy when I finally get it to him, palm up flat, of course. I rub my hand over the star on his forehead, and then on his neck. My fingers are steady, calm. I can feel Duke's breath, like my breath, moving in and out at different times, his enormous weight leaning into my hand just the right amount. It feels safe—like when people tell you to calm down, this is what that calm might actually feel like. It feels like the opposite of the Gray.

Duke finishes the apple and walks toward the other side of the stall. Then he stops, lifts his tail, and lets it all out. I shovel it the best I can into the blue bin, trying not to get any of it on me. "Duke, how does your hay turn into all this?" Duke puts his muzzle against my chest. "Don't try to make me feel better." But I do feel better. "Eli's my bodyguard, Duke. He's strong like you are, and he tries to act tough, but he's actually pretty nice." Duke walks slowly to the outside part of his stall. I follow him. He stares out into the mist. "I think he misses Jesse. Duke, did you know Jesse?"

"Ready to clean his hooves?" Eli comes into the stall holding a silver hook-shaped thing about the size of his hand.

"I guess?" I say.

"Here you go." He hands me the hook. "We have to clean out their hooves because stuff gets all caught up inside of them." I stare at Duke's hooves. "First thing to do is to get right here . . ." He wedges himself against Duke, then reaches down and pulls on the hairs right above his hoof. "Give a little pull on the fetlock right here . . ." He tugs the hair, and Duke folds his leg up so the hoof rests neatly under Eli's arm. "Then you take the hook and scrape out the mud and gunk." As he does this, huge chunks of mud come flying out.

He puts the hoof down, and I walk to the other side. "Okay, Duke, we can do this." I try tugging the hairs, but Duke won't lift his leg. I try again, and nothing. Eli walks over.

"Are you even trying? Here." He lowers his head. "Pull my hair as hard as you're pulling Duke's. Let me see." I pull lightly. "C'mon!" Eli says. "Give it a real pull. This is a horse!" So I pull harder, and just like that, Duke's hoof comes right up under my arm and is resting on my knee. I feel him right above me, so calm and trusting. Slowly, I pick the mud and hay out of his hoof. It comes out in huge chunks until it's cleaned out.

I know I need to get back soon. Aunt Ruthie gives me so much freedom. More than I have ever had before, but it's getting late. I don't want to leave, though. The horses feel like guardians, like they won't let anything happen to me, like they are *all* my bodyguards. I don't know when I started to feel this way, but I feel it now—it's almost overpowering. "One more thing," Eli says. "Take Duke for a walk."

"A walk?"

"Yeah, he didn't go on any rides today. He needs to stretch his legs." Eli hooks a long rope to a thin gray halter. "Just walk over to the ring and come back. Maybe once around the barn?"

I walk Duke out into the open. I don't have to pull him; he feels weightless as he walks with me, step by step. He stops when I stop. Every so often he leans down toward a patch of green clover. "We did this before, didn't we? We are good at walking. Sorry I didn't get back on that day. It's complicated." We go around the barn where we feel the open air of the wide pasture, the drizzle turning into rain. I feel so small next to him. I feel like I am my actual size. Small. And next to Duke, it's okay to be small. The hair on Duke's back shines in the late afternoon sun. I imagine a saddle and me in the saddle trying to ride him again. But when I do, I feel breathless.

"See, Duke, sometimes I go into this place—at least I think it's a place. Maybe it's in my mind, but it's all cloudy and full of shadows. Sometimes it's hard to see. Sometimes

I see too much . . ." Duke tightens up. A white dog with one blue eye stops in its tracks and starts barking. I feel a slight pull on the lead, but Duke doesn't run. He settles down and gets nearer to me, like he knows that I might be afraid— like he can feel me.

"Good dog," I say. I wave my hand over the dog's head like I'm doing a Jedi mind trick. "This is not the horse you're looking for . . ." It starts licking my hand and rolling over in the dirt. Duke leans his muzzle into my shoulder. I turn to look him in his enormous eye. "Want to take a ride together one day?" That's when I see, at the farthest edge of the fence, the dark shape of Eli standing inside the fence line next to a tall horse. It's the Gray. He's feeding her, or maybe talking to her?

"See that, Duke?" Duke doesn't move. Eli puts his hand on the horse's neck, gently reaches to the ground, and then lifts something up. A saddle. She backs off, her black mane whipping in the wet air. But she calms down as Eli gets closer. "I think Eli's going to ride her, Duke." Duke shows me his big yellow-and-white teeth. I lead him back to the barn. I take off the halter and lead. I'm getting better at doing this. Duke trots over to the water trough and takes a long, slow drink. Then I lead him into his stall. "See you soon, Duke," I whisper. "Thanks."

When I turn around, Eli is already putting the saddle back on the rack with all the others.

"Did you ride her? How was it? Me and Duke got in trouble with a dog, but it was cool." Eli just looks at me.

"I didn't ride her yet. Saddle only today. Hey, it's getting late."

I grab my stuff, ready to head out. When I'm almost out of the barn, I hear Eli call out, "You know, right? About the Gray?"

I stop, then turn around, surprised to hear those words coming out of Eli's mouth. But of course he means his horse.

"The Gray. She's Jesse's horse. She's always been Jesse's. Nobody's ridden her since . . . since . . . Since Jesse's been gone, no one has been able to ride her. She gallops like a wild gray ghost through the pastures. Everyone just started calling her the Gray. Her real name is Star."

I think of a million things to say—but what comes out is a nod and the words, "I understand."

He shakes his head. "One thing at a time, for both of us? Maybe riding is for tomorrow."

Star thunders through the grass, galloping along the fence—a gray storm cloud against the green fields. I wave to her, then make my way to the forest path, where the rain falls in oversize drops into the pond full of croaking frogs, and up to the house where Aunt Ruthie is sitting on the porch, waiting for me.

"Hey, kiddo." Aunt Ruthie lifts a plate of chocolate chip cookies. I grab two and sit in the old chair next to her. "What in the world?" She pinches her nose and looks me up and down. "You are something else right now, my boy."

I realize that my shoes are muddy, and my shorts and shirt are covered in hay and who knows what else. I need to wash my hands, but it feels really good to sit. I tell Aunt Ruthie about my day, about Duke and Eli. I can't remember the last time I've been this tired, and it feels good. "Wait a minute," she says. "Is that a smile under all the sludge? Could it be that all this fresh air and outdoor life are doing you some good?"

I thought coming here would mean being bored and doing nothing, but so far, it's been the opposite of that. If I wasn't smiling before, I am now.

In the morning, we are fishing again, me and Ivy and Eli. But we can't catch anything because Ivy decides to swim. "I'm saving these poor fish from you monsters," she says. Eli tries anyway.

After, Ivy even walks with us through the forest and past the pond—where the frogs are more awake than ever because it's been so rainy. "Hold on," she says. Then she gets down low and creeps along the bank, waits, and then jumps forward. When she gets up, her pants are all muddy and she has a tiny green-and-black spotted frog in her hand. "Look at this wee one," she says. She puts it up to her face so she's nose to nose with it. "He matches my hair! I'm gonna call you Jumpers!"

I look at the Stone of Power. It seems brighter. Maybe the rain over the past few days has cleaned it a bit. Every part of it shimmers in the morning sunlight that's seeping through the trees. I think of Uncle Lou and try to do what he always said: Take it all in. Feel grounded.

We walk together past the ranch. Eli stops to say hello to Star, who waits for him by the fence and whinnies wildly when we have to leave her. Ivy lets Jumpers ride on her shoulder or in her pocket the whole way to town. When we get there, Ivy takes Jumpers over to the park while Eli and I go to the gym. We practice something new today: somersaults. We take turns rolling across the mats. We pretend that someone has pushed us from behind, then we practice the way our hands should land, how to tuck our chins to our chests and roll onto our shoulders. The first time I try it, I land flat on my back, but after a while it gets better, until I can do two or three in a row. "Practice is key," Nate says. "Before today, a lot of you never thought you could do this at all. See? Just a little at a time." In the corner, Eli is roundhouse kicking the heavy bag until I think it might explode.

After class we see Ivy across the street at the park, but she isn't alone. Ally, Johnny, and Oscar are there in a big clump. "Do you think she's okay?" I ask. Eli doesn't respond. "I mean, she's friends with them, right?" But that's when we hear her yelling something. We run across the street, and when we get there, the group backs away a little.

"Give him to me!" Ivy yells. Her sleeves are covered in dirt. Boon walks up from the baseball field holding a bat in one hand, his mitt tucked under his arm.

"She took Jumpers!" Ivy yells, her eyes pleading.

"I did not!" Ally screams as she holds a scared-looking Jumpers in her hands. "I found a frog. It's not my fault you think it's yours."

"It's just a stupid frog, right?" Boon says. "What's the big deal?"

"He needs to go home to his pond!" Ivy shouts. "Give him back!" Ivy rushes at Ally, who steps next to Boon.

"C'mon," I say, trying to be calm. "Can you just give Ivy her frog back?"

"No way, Squishy—and back off," Ally says, the others laughing at the nickname. "You're not even from here. You don't know how it works with frogs."

Whether out of frustration, or fear, or something else entirely, Ivy starts crying. "I have to take him back. I promised I would." And for the first time, I see Boon's face change. Does he feel bad for Ivy?

"Ally," Boon says, "can you just give her the frog?"

"Jumpers," Ivy says through tears.

"What a dumb name," Ally says, staring at the frog. "He's too fat. I'll call him Plumpers. I bet my cat would love to play with Plumpers." She makes a claw out of her hand and takes a fake swipe. Ivy lunges to snatch Jumpers out of Ally's hands, but Ally moves out of the way and almost trips, her hands opening wide enough for Jumpers to escape. Suddenly free, he leaps away through the grass. The rest of us rush together to try to stop Ally and Ivy from fighting, but we smash together in a big clump, everyone yelling over the next person.

I recognize this feeling. Being trapped. Bodies pressing. Hands reaching and pulling. All I want to do is fight my way out. I start pushing as hard as I can against the person nearest to me. Boon. He grabs my arm, pulling me with him to the ground. My face lands in the grass. I can taste it. Boon gets up, but before he can do anything, Eli reaches in and lifts Boon up by his arm. But it's not just a pull; it's some kind of grab. He's bending Boon's hand back in a way that forces Boon to lean forward.

"Get off me," Boon says. "I wasn't doing anything—I was trying to help."

But Eli doesn't let go, and I know Boon is feeling the pressure. He's sweating, even turning red as Eli holds his arm. "Guys!" Ivy calls out. She waves to us, holding Jumpers in her other hand. Eli lets go, and I see tears in the corners of Boon's eyes. He looks at us, his face bright red, then wipes the dirt and mud off his baseball uniform.

"We don't need this," Boon says. "What happened to you, Eli? You think by protecting these losers you can make up for what happened?"

Eli stares at him. Boon avoids his gaze.

"Let's go," Boon says. He walks back toward the baseball field. Ally and Oscar go slowly, looking at Ivy and then over at us like they want to say something, but they don't. We get our stuff together. Ivy pats the dirt and mud off of herself the best she can. She talks to Jumpers, who is nestled inside her closed hand, and we start back up the path away from town.

None of us say anything. Right now, there's nothing to say.

The drizzle makes the trail muddier than ever. Ivy carries Jumpers the whole way. He looks terrified, frozen like a fake frog in her hand. "Don't worry," she says. "We're taking you home." We drop Eli off at the ranch, and I agree to come back right after I go with Ivy to take Jumpers back to the pond.

We find our way through the forest between the shimmering beech trees, to where the pond is alive with tiny raindrops. The frogs are all out, singing wildly in the wet afternoon. "They're singing for you, Jumpers. Sorry I took you away from your home, and for what happened at the park. I hope it was an interesting adventure." Jumpers doesn't move. He hasn't moved the whole walk home. He looks like a little frog statue. We walk to where we found him and kneel on the grass by the edge of the pond. Ivy rests her hand in the soft earth, but Jumpers doesn't move. I wonder if he's scared. If he goes back to his pond life, will it feel the same? He's a different frog now. He's been through so much. What if he doesn't want to do the same frog things as before?

Ivy's so patient, waiting to see what happens. Then, one by one, we see little light-bulb eyes coming out of the water. They're watching, and occasionally a bubble is blown or a croak is croaked. Jumpers inches forward. Ivy looks at me, and by the time she looks back, Jumpers is off and into the water with a *plop*.

Ivy watches the frogs for a while, then dips her hands into the pond. "I'm supposed to go dance with Ruthie, but I don't feel like dancing today. Will you walk me there so I can tell her?"

I walk her all the way to the door, even though I need to get back to the ranch to help Eli. "I'm sorry about what happened," I say quietly. "I have to get to the ranch, but . . ."

"It's okay," she says. "Some days just aren't for dancing. I'll be okay."

46

The forest air is thick and damp. I take slow steps through the mist. It almost feels like the Gray is taking over the whole world, but I can feel my fingertips, my breath, and I know where my steps are taking me—just one at a time, the forest winding down the hill to where the ranch spreads into the pastures. I'm excited to see Duke. Maybe not so excited to shovel more horse poop, but it doesn't matter, because when I finally get close enough, I see something that changes everything.

47

Eli is standing with Star in the farthest pasture. The saddle is on the ground, but he's put a bridle on her. I walk up and lean on the fence. He lifts a blanket and puts it on Star's back, then rubs her neck and quietly whispers, "Good girl."

"You're gonna ride?" I say. I have so many questions about what made him want to try it now, but I hold on to them. Instead, I say, "I bet this would make Jesse happy." Eli stops, turns around, and looks straight at me, his curly hair drooping down in the drizzle. I can't tell if he's mad or sad. He turns back and continues to tack her up.

"Do you know what *actually* happened?" Eli says, not looking at me.

"I don't know too much. It seems like nobody does. Just bits and pieces of the story," I say. Eli stops.

"I want to tell you," he says, and then, so quietly that I almost don't hear him, "I need to tell someone." I feel words and ideas bubbling up and almost flowing out of me. I want to ask questions, but instead I breathe. I listen.

● ● ● ● ● ●

"I just went up to the hayloft that day, you know, to see if I left my gloves on the haystacks. I was going to say hi to Jesse because he was being really quiet. Usually he asks nonstop questions—kind of like someone else I know." He looks over at me. "I thought I would check in, maybe see what he was reading, or if he needed any help with his homework. Sometimes he gets stuck in reading. He doesn't always pay attention. Like he's in another world." Eli steps toward the fence and leans his head down on the post.

"Eli, I . . ." I try to say something.

"You should have seen him, Sasha. When I found him that day, he was covered in hay, crying on the floor of the loft. Then there was Tommy, the horse trainer, standing above him, looking at me with hollow eyes. I don't know exactly what he did to Jesse. At first, I was scared, really scared. I felt every part of me start to slip away, and it felt like everything in the barn was suddenly different. Tommy didn't even look like a person. He looked like some kind of monster, bent over, dark shadows on his face. And Jesse . . . he was so pale. Tommy smiled when he saw me. He just smiled. It was wicked. Worse than Boon, worse than anything you've ever seen. Like a nightmare come to life." Eli kicks the fence post with his hard boot, and I feel it vibrate. "I should have been there sooner. I could have stopped him."

I feel the air around us get a little colder. "But what did you do?" I whisper.

"When he smiled like that, something came over me. I

couldn't even feel anything until my elbows hit his head and my feet slipped on the hay, all my weight pressing him down, and then suddenly he was gone, falling back. I heard his body slam onto the floor below."

Star walks toward the fence. She looks peaceful, her deep brown eyes open wide. Gently, she pushes her nose into Eli's face.

Eli is quiet for a while. Then he starts back up.

"Everyone says that *I'm* crazy, that my brother had to move away because *I'm a threat* and that *I* might hurt him or my family." Eli looks up, his face full of tears and snot. "I'm *not* a threat!" he yells. "I'm not the one. I protected him. I'm not the threat. I should have known that Tommy was a bad guy. Why didn't I know sooner? I didn't want him to fall out of the hayloft. But he had no right . . ." He stops, tries to breathe, and I recognize the pattern, box breaths, the same ones I practice all the time. Slow—in and out—on purpose.

Every day I wish I hadn't lashed out and hurt Jeremy. Eli wishes that he'd done something sooner to help his brother. Is there a way to get through things without wanting to hit the replay button?

"Jesse went with our mom to California to get away from this town. From the memories of what he went through. To get help. Not to get away from me. He's coming back someday. Soon! But no one cares about that. People see the world how they want to."

"I believe you," I say.

Eli looks up. He wipes his nose with his jacket, then reaches down and grabs the saddle from both sides and, in one strong motion, he swings it up and over Star's back and onto the blanket with a *thwump*.

"So where are you gonna ride?" I ask. He cinches the saddle and feels the give.

"I'm not," he says, putting his hands on the reins. "You are."

48

I squeeze the fence. Me? My heart beats faster. I look up at the gray sky, feel my feet in the dirt.

"But what about you?" I say, trying not to show my nervousness.

"I've been riding my whole life." Eli puts his hands on the pommel. "It's time for you to get back on the horse, I guess. Don't worry, I'll lead her the whole time." All this seems like too big of a step, too much at once. I look down toward the barn and think of Duke. What if I went to get him? Star sighs deeply, then puts her head over the fence, her silvery-gray hair shining in the light drizzle.

I think of my aunt Ruthie: *When things feel big, take them just one step at a time.* I think I can do this. So I do. I climb over the fence and down the other side. I tighten my backpack straps. I walk up to Star and smile, letting her know that I'm ready because I've learned that horses can read minds, or at least emotions.

"I can do this, Star," I say to her. Eli reaches down to hold the stirrup so I can put my foot in. I fit it in, pressing down on it with my toe and lifting myself up and over until I land squarely in the saddle.

Being on Duke felt like sitting on top of the Stone of Power—solid. But Star feels different, like floating on a canoe that might take off at any moment. I feel my stomach churning as she leans side to side, antsy, ready to run.

"Hold on to the saddle," Eli says. "I've got the reins."

Step by step, Eli leads us out into the pastures.

49

Riding Duke felt like what I imagine it would be like to ride in a landspeeder—smooth and rhythmic. It was hard not to want to close my eyes. With Star, I feel every thundering step. We walk through the open pasture, Eli carefully holding the reins.

"Is she okay?" I ask, my voice shaking with every step.

Eli looks back. I can tell he's double-checking everything. I hold on extra tight.

"She's just fine. Are you okay up there?" he says.

I'm still nervous. I hold on a little tighter. I remember talking to Dr. W about *the mind-body connection*. Even if I feel fear in my body, I can try to have peace in my mind. I breathe and try to let my fear change to peace, and before I know it, we are up on the gravel road near Aunt Ruthie's house. I can see smoke rising from the chimney and silhouettes through the window. I want to yell for them to look at us.

We walk faster, the rain a steady drizzle, and soon we see the sign for Camp Akiva and the old road. Through the gate, I see the spot from the first day where I tripped and Ivy helped me up.

"We're going down this hill. Lean way back," Eli says. I do, leaning so far back it feels like I might just lie down. Eventually the path evens out, and we walk across the camp— through the big meadow and past the lake and the dock where we fish, and then by the old boathouse where I threw up on Boon and a baseball field overgrown with weeds. "I want to show you something," Eli says. We go past the last bunkhouse in the row, Bunk 14. At the very end is a small barn about the size of one of the bunkhouses.

"What is that?" I ask.

"This is one of Jesse's favorite places. It's where they kept some of the animals: sheep, goats, chickens. We would come and visit the animals. Some of the animals were still here after the camp closed down, until they found them a home."

"They did find them a home, right?" I ask.

"They did, but it's weird. Even when the animals were gone, we still came by here to explore and stuff. We used to come at night and take turns going inside the barn, alone, for as long as we could."

"Why would *anyone* do that?" I say.

"The freakiest part for me was that sometimes we would still hear animal noises from the empty barn. Who knows what lives in there."

I stare at the barn, listening as hard as I can. I take deep breaths and focus on what's safe, what's real.

Eli leads us down the row of bunkhouses. I imagine kids playing, and all the life that must have been here. I think about Aunt Ruthie and Uncle Lou, and how they probably went into all these cabins, helping kids have fun or comforting them when they missed their family. But now, in the gray afternoon, the doors are mostly pulled off the hinges and the glass broken out of every window. The rain starts to fall heavier—I can see the drops now. Step by step we get closer to the barn at the end of the row. The barn doors are half open, light pouring through the cracks of the splintered wood into the darkened space.

I get down off Star. It feels so good to put my feet on the ground. Eli ties her to a post outside the barn and whispers, "Good girl. Sorry I haven't been riding. I miss Jesse. I know you do, too." She puts her muzzle in his face. He pulls an apple from his jacket pocket, and she chomps it down. All around us the bunks feel like a forgotten village, the trees soaring above their roofs.

"What do we do now?" I ask. Eli smiles at me and points to the barn, but then we hear a *squawk* from inside, and what sounds like the fluttering of wings, and then another *squawk*!

50

The squawks get louder. Star swishes her tail back and forth and grinds her teeth, her front legs drumming into the dirt. Eli steps back, and so do I. A crashing noise sounds from inside, like something huge fell over, and then we hear something else—a low and sudden growl, like some giant beast? Something's coming out.

My breath changes. It feels like the world shifts and peels back. The bunkhouses darken into shadowy caves, and the barn soars above us like a mountain. I try to breathe through it, stunned at how quickly it came on. Only this time, Eli is right next to me. He looks at me, everything moving in what feels like slow motion. I hear the squawk again, deeper this time. Eli points up to a window in the loft of the barn, and we see something—not shadowy, but bright? A person? Or something else looking out the window, extending a long arm, and urgently pointing down? Then suddenly, along with the sound of flapping and squawking, giant birds fly out of the high window and into the swirling skies. I stare at the shadowy birds against the grayness, feel the wind blowing steadily, and can't stop staring until I feel the heavy weight of Eli's hand on my arm. When I turn toward him, he's yelling something—my name?—but it sounds like he's screaming into a pillow. I see Star behind him. I find a breath and then another, and all at once, the sound comes back.

"*Sasha!*" he says.

Star is spooked. She lifts her front legs, neighing loudly, her mane wild. Eli tries to get her to calm down. I duck into the doorway of one of the bunks and sit down, pulling my knees to my chest. Through the doorway I see something else coming out of the barn—but they aren't birds, or animals at all. They're human shapes. One by one, they come out, and that's when we realize.

It's Boon.

Boon, Ally, Johnny, and Oscar, laughing as they spill out of the barn doors.

"You were so scared!" They point at Eli and then Star, who's rearing now, lifting her front legs higher, arching her neck toward the sky. Ally sees me in the doorway.

"Come out, Squishy," she says.

"What do you guys want?" I yell. They come closer to Eli, their hands in fists.

"What's wrong, Eli? Did you think it was a ghost? I thought you were so tough. You afraid of ghosts?"

But Eli ignores them. He's focused on Star. Her chest heaves in and out. She whinnies loudly, her tail swishing fast. Her hooves slam into the trembling ground.

Boon walks over to me. "You know what I just realized?" He looks around at the others. "Maybe Squishy here is taking the place of Jesse."

"Stop it, Boon!" I yell.

"Is that right, Eli? Your own brother is too scared to be around you so you got this weirdo to be like your new little brother?"

Eli holds Star's reins, trying to steady her.

"Is it true, Eli? Is this your new brother? You even got him to ride his wild horse?" He raises his hands into the air, making his fingers into claws, and lets out a loud growl like he's emptying out everything inside of him, then lunges at Star.

That's all she can take. Star lifts her front legs high above our heads. Boon and the others cower while Eli tries to get ahold of the reins. Johnny gets behind me, grabs my arms. I try to wrestle myself out of his grasp by kicking against his legs, but he's too big. There's so much noise, Star's whinnying turning to shrieking, and then out of nowhere I see Boon running at me. He puts his hands out and pushes me in the chest. It feels like a cannonball.

I   *can't*   *breathe.*

My vision blurs, but I see Eli drop Star's reins and run at Boon, lifting his big boot and landing his heel right into Boon's side. Boon goes flying, then crashes to the ground. Everyone's shouting, louder and louder until the sound is like walls all around me. I try to suck in air, but it feels like it's coming through a straw. Star's bridle goes flying, the saddle starting to slip from her back. She raises her hooves high in the air again, whinnying into the gray sky. Eli turns and tries to reach her, but Boon is already up, and while Eli's back is turned, Boon pushes him. Eli falls forward, his head snapping back from the blow, and lands in the mud. He paws at the ground, still crawling toward Star, but it's too late. She's free. Star turns toward the barn and takes off, her feet cutting into the mud, her hooves like drumbeats on the wet earth. She flies past the barn, and before she reaches the trees, the saddle unhitches all the way and falls to the ground. Star lets out a loud whinny, then bolts into the forest, like a gray spirit in the trees.

51

Eli stays still on the ground, and for a moment, everything is silent. Sometimes sound doesn't seem real until it's not there anymore.

"Come on, get up!" Boon shouts. "You're not so tough now." Ally and the others don't say anything. They look off to where Star disappeared into the trees.

I want Eli to get up, to take Boon down Jedi-style. But he doesn't move.

I shake my arms wildly, trying again to break free from Johnny's hold. This time, though, Johnny loosens his grip, then lets go, and I hear him whisper something that sounds like "Sorry."

I rush over to Eli.

"Eli! Are you okay?" I say. His head is still down, his face half in the mud, and he's looking toward the trees. "Can you get up?" I ask. He looks at me, his face tight, his eyes lost. Then he starts to stand.

"It's about time!" says Boon.

Eli straightens up and shakes off some mud.

Boon walks over to where we're standing. "C'mon, let's do this," he yells, his face right next to Eli's.

"Boon, cut it out," Ally says. Everyone's mood has changed. Eli takes a step, then another, and then takes off running, as fast as he can, past the barn and into the forest where Star went, his green jacket flying behind him.

"That's right!" Boon calls after him. "Just run away!" Then he turns and lunges at me, catching me off guard. I get myself into a defensive stance, but I slip back onto the wet ground, my hands planted into the mud. The four of them stand over me, and I feel for my breath. It's hard to get control of it. My stomach hurts. The world is turning gray.

52

The world is mist. It feels like the half-asleep, half-awake place. Not the Gray completely, but somewhere in between? I still hear them talking.

"What do we do, Boon?" Ally asks.

"Shut up," Boon says. "Let me think."

"Maybe we need to help—now!" Johnny says.

I feel a hand on my shoulder. "Are you okay?" Johnny whispers to me through the half-light. I don't say anything. Or I can't—I'm not sure. I hear a loud sound, like thunder booming.

"Oh no!" Ally yells. Her voice is piercing. Then the voices of the others ring out.

"Let's get out of here!"

"Let's go!"

The thundering sound gets louder and closer, and there are other noises, too. I lift my head to see what's happening. Lights swallow the darkness—some giant thing has come. I open my eyes wide. A truck door slams, then I see something familiar. It's Ivy on one side and Aunt Ruthie on the other, swinging her cane in the air.

Ivy is yelling, too.

Boon and the others are already on their bikes, riding fast through the trees. I'm covered in mud. My shirt is ripped, but I'm coming to my senses.

"Sasha, what in the world is happening?" Aunt Ruthie wipes her hand across my muddy forehead. "Were you fighting with those boys? Are you all right?" She looks up and shakes her cane into the wind.

"Let's get you out of the mud," Ivy says, offering her hand. I put all the energy I can find into grabbing her hand, into moving my legs, into sitting up and finally standing.

"Thanks," I say, trying to scrape the mud off, but I'm just making it worse.

"Sasha," Aunt Ruthie says, leaning over her cane and pacing back and forth. She sounds serious. "We need to know what's going on here."

The warm rain starts to come down harder now, silvery streaks in the headlights.

"Hey," Ivy says, looking around. "Is Eli here with you?" I look out at the forest.

"Out there. He's out there." I point to the forest. Ivy runs toward the trees and looks around, but it's already getting way too dark.

53

We are all silent on the ride home. I think about how nothing is ever really within our control, but somehow, even in the quiet of the truck, just being here with Aunt Ruthie and Ivy makes me feel like maybe things will be okay. When we get home, I shower and change out of my muddy clothes.

"I'll call Eli's father and Jake at the ranch to make sure they know what's going on. Don't worry," she says. "He'll be fine."

But how can she know?

Aunt Ruthie disappears for a little while. When she comes back, her face looks normal again. Relaxed.

"They are all aware," she says calmly, "and are already out looking for them. It's just the rainy night that makes it hard." Then it's silent for a few moments. Aunt Ruthie turns on the kettle and gets out some big mugs. She mixes us hot chocolate with whipped cream piled high, then retrieves a bag of marshmallows, rips it open, and lets them pour out like a waterfall. "This is a situation that requires many marshmallows," she says.

Aunt Ruthie paces in the kitchen while I tell her and Ivy what happened. I try my best to explain, and they are patient with me as the words tumble out. Ivy squashes marshmallows one by one, then drops them into her cocoa. Ivy tells us how mad she is, and I try to tell them that I'm worried about Eli—and Star. Through tears and squashed marshmallows, we agree that we all are.

"He'll be okay," Aunt Ruthie says. "He'll make it home. And so will the horse."

After a long, tired silence, Aunt Ruthie says, "You know what else this requires?" She goes to her record player and puts on an old, scratchy record. Then she curtsies to Ivy, like some secret language between best friends. They face each other, then start dancing together across the living room. The sound of drums and horns fills the air. They're smiling in the warm lamplight. And even though things feel out of control, I still feel safe.

Ivy holds out her hand. I get up reluctantly at first, but then I start to move my legs. Aunt Ruthie grabs my other hand, and they spin me around and we bounce up and down to the music until we fall onto the couches, exhausted.

"C'mon, we need to get Ivy home. Will you put her bike in the truck?"

We drive down the wet roads. Ivy and I sit in the back seat.

"I wish I could have been there with you guys," Ivy says. "Boon has always been arrogant, and a bully, but I think for some reason, seeing you with Eli, actually being friends? I think it made him more of a jerk."

"What? Why?" I say.

"Duh," she says, tucking her hair behind her ears.

"Sorry," I say. "I'm still thinking about what happened."

"It's just that when all that stuff happened with Jesse, Boon actually tried to stick up for Eli. *He's* the one who tried to tell everyone that it was an accident. He used to say that Eli would never do something like that on purpose—attack someone—unless Jesse was in trouble. But nobody knew what to think or who to listen to."

It makes sense. I got so mad at Jeremy that I hit him in the head with my math book. Of course, it wasn't okay for those kids to crowd in on me like that—to treat me that way. But mainly I was hurt, confused. It felt like I lost someone, and I didn't understand it. I've been annoyed at Daniel and my parents before, but it's hard to tell them how I feel. It's much easier to ignore them, to hide.

We drive past the ranch, the dull yellow light through the barn windows pouring out into the dark. I think about Duke resting inside. I wonder if he knows that Star is gone. Horses can feel human emotions, like fear. They must feel each other's. But then I have a thought.

"Do horses find their way home?"

"What?" Ivy says.

"Do horses find their way home—if they get lost?"

"Perhaps," Aunt Ruthie says. "They are very intelligent

beasts." I strain my eyes, looking out toward the far fences where Star might be. Maybe she came back, but it's too dark to see for sure.

"How about we check tomorrow, and we can look for Eli back at the camp? Maybe at the fishing dock tomorrow morning?" Ivy smiles.

"Good plan," I say. But it's tonight I'm worried about.

54

I take my medicine and practice my breathing, but I can't sleep. I am too worried about Eli.

Not sleeping makes things worse. Dr. Winters told me that not sleeping is one of the most dangerous things for me. When I'm tired, the "door" to the Gray seems to open more easily. He told me that too much time on a screen affects how we sleep. It's been better since I've been here. I've had fewer nightmares, slept better. But not tonight. I hear Aunt Ruthie's music downstairs and try to focus on its rhythms. I take out my pad and draw the Stone of Power. I stare at the beams on the ceiling and count the knotholes until they look like they're floating off the wood. The trees sway in the moonlight outside my window. My eyelids get heavier and heavier and heavier. I put my hand on my heart and suddenly gasp—like I forgot how to breathe. Somewhere between asleep and awake, I open my eyes into a dream, but it seems so real.

I'm standing in a wide field with a forest of shadowy trees bending behind me. It's light enough out to see. I look around. It's a place I've never been. I smell wet earth, feel a cool breeze on my skin. I try to walk, but my legs feel like they are tied to bricks. In the center of the meadow is a large, round stone. I drag myself over to it and sit. The meadow spreads toward the forest, where the light gray turns darker. I put my head in my hands, rub my eyes to see more clearly. Something is standing at the far edge of the meadow, just past the place where the shadow trees begin. Is it a deer? Or maybe a coyote? No, it's something else. Whatever it is, it sees me, and suddenly lurches into the meadow, coming right toward me. I stand up, my heart beating faster in the cold air. The ghostly shape gets closer, and as it does, something else happens. There's a loud noise, like someone yelling into a megaphone from some-where far away. I cover my ears, shut my eyes tight, and squeeze my whole body, breathless.

When I open my eyes, light floods the room. It must be morning? Aunt Ruthie is sitting at the edge of the bed with her usual tea steaming from her blue-and-white Camp Akiva cup.

"It's okay, Sasha," she says. She gently squeezes my hand and waits for me to wake up a little more.

"I had a bad dream," I say, sitting up. "I was in the Gray, and there was someone there with me. I saw them in a meadow! The whole place seemed familiar, but I've never been there before."

"Breathe, my little Jedi."

I do.

"I know about these kinds of dreams, Sasha. Uncle Lou has, I mean *had*, those dreams all the time. They were so real for him that he sometimes didn't know what was real or what was a dream. But when he woke up, he often felt like he just lived through something special, maybe even important."

"What did he do?" I ask. She stares into her cup.

"For him, it was the place where all the worlds of water and woods came together. He said that in that place, all the hidden things didn't have to hide. *Worlds within worlds*, he would say. I'm not sure what all that means, but I *do* know that he used to see things, or places he'd never been, and then one day we'd be walking somewhere, and he would know all about it, like he'd been there many times before."

"So for him it was real?" I ask.

"As real as anything else, but he learned how to tell the difference. He accepted it. After a while, he stopped trying to explain it all away. He acknowledged that it was a gift, a good part of who he was, and it didn't make sense to try to change it."

"Was it the medicine that helped him?" I ask.

"He took it, yes, but the medicine was just part of it. He had me, the camp, his community, breathing, and routine, and all the good things in the world to help him, too."

I look up. "Like how for a Jedi, the lightsaber is only one

part of who they are. But they have all the Force abilities, too."

"YES!" Aunt Ruthie says. "Just like a Jedi. Yoda has his lightsaber, but it's just one part of his story." She stands up. "Join me downstairs when you're ready."

● ● ● ● ● ●

When I go downstairs for breakfast, Aunt Ruthie's on the phone. I watch her twist the weird spirally cord of her old phone around her finger, then she hangs up and slides a plate of toast with cream cheese in front of me.

"He didn't come home, Sasha."

"What?"

"I talked to Jake at the ranch, and Eli's father. Eli hasn't come home yet."

"No!" I say, pushing my finger straight into my toast.

"The other thing is that Star isn't back yet, either, *but* . . ." She shifts her voice into a nice, calm tone, the voice she uses when she's about to get to the good part of a story. "Jake is taking a group back out to look for them. So is Sheriff Hett and everyone else. They will find him."

I stare at my toast. I feel relieved that everyone is going to look for him, but I also feel something else.

"What should *I* do?"

Aunt Ruthie looks around.

"Well," she says. "Ivy's coming over in a little while. Maybe you two can join in with everyone later on?"

I nod.

"But how about you take a bite of that, um, smashed toast and get some food in your belly first." I look outside at the blue sky while I eat. It's stopped raining and is summery again. *At least he won't be wet*, I think.

55

When Ivy arrives, she has some toast and cream cheese, too.

"We should go look for Eli at the camp," she says.

"Is it safe?" I ask.

"It'll be okay," she says. "We'll check for him now while the sun is out, and then we can meet up with everyone later."

"Unless we find him at the camp first!" I smile. We tell Aunt Ruthie our plan. She makes us promise not to stay too long and to join up with everyone else after.

"Who knows," Ivy says. "Maybe he's just there fishing at the dock like always?" The sun is bright, pushing all the clouds from the sky. We make our way to the camp and through the meadow toward the lake.

"No deer today," she says.

"Wait," I whisper, and stop in the middle of the trail. "Look." Ivy silently claps her hands with joy. There, just inside the tree line, we see deer mixed in with the forest, perfectly blending in with the tree bark and dappled sunlight.

For a moment, I see a stag deeper in the trees. He turns his huge antlers toward us, his eyes shining in the unearthly light. "They're almost invisible," I say.

"They're wild," she hums. We walk quietly on until we can see the dock. Eli isn't there, and we are surprised to see bikes parked at the entrance of the camp. Two people are walking back from the far end. My heart leaps for a moment, but then we see that it's Johnny and Oscar.

"What are they doing here?" I sneer, but by now Ivy has almost reached them.

"Why are you guys even here?" she asks.

Johnny steps over. "It's okay. Sorry, Ivy. Eli's dad called all our parents. Asked us to help find him. We've looked everywhere we can think of."

"Why do *you* suddenly care?" Ivy crosses her arms and looks at the two boys.

"It went too far," Oscar adds. "And sorry, Squishy, about yesterday."

I look at him. "It's Sasha," I say.

56

We walk around the camp with Johnny and Oscar. At first, we keep our distance from them, but eventually it just feels like four kids looking for something impossible to find. We search the old bunkhouses, the rec room, and even a broken-down workshop before we find our way over to an old white building with a giant barn door that's been slid open. The inside of the building is lined with high shelves that stretch across the whole place. Old trunks lay open and empty on the floor, everything ransacked. But the floor looks alive because there are raccoons crawling everywhere. They scatter and hiss at us when we first come in, like little goblins going in and out of dark holes. I think about ghosts, and about Miriam, the lost girl that Ivy and Aunt Ruthie talked about, but I don't say anything.

"This place is messed up," Oscar says. "It gives me the creeps. There's nothing here but raccoons and old luggage. I say we get out of here."

Johnny looks from side to side, then back to the door. "There's a search party setting out from the ranch later. You gonna join?" he asks.

"Of course we are!" Ivy promises.

"Cool," says Johnny. "We'll see you there."

They leave and Ivy points to a raccoon that's crawling along a high loft beneath the light of a broken window. "I wish we could search from a really high place, too, you know? Look down on everything." Right as she says this, we hear a crashing sound a few rows over. "What was that?" Ivy asks, her eyes searching.

"Probably more raccoons, right?" I say nervously.

Then we hear another sound, like a whistle, or maybe even a voice?

"Is someone over there?" I call out, my heart rate spiking.

Ivy crosses her arms. "Wait," she says. "It's okay. Raccoons can make noises that sound like people. There must be a lot of them around." We hear a loud creak, and all of a sudden, one of the old trunks comes crashing down from the loft and lands right in front of us. We jump back. Dirt and dust fly into the air, and the trunk, which is turned on its side, is spewing papers and old photos across the ground.

"Wow," Ivy says, shaking off the dust from the trunk. "Look at this." She points to the papers and photos, torn and browned with age. She reaches down to pick some of them up but gasps loudly, suddenly falling back. A raccoon cub springs out from the inside of the trunk and runs between our legs. I watch it scurry off into the building, and that's when I feel something I've never felt before. A cold chill passes through me from back to front, toward where the trunk sits on the ground. For a moment, the air around us shimmers. It's like something is here. Or maybe it's all the dust in the air. My breathing is shallow. I rub my eyes, and when I stop, things feel normal again.

Ivy kneels in the pile of papers. Sunlight pours through the high window, right onto where she sorts the old, faded photographs, mostly of kids with their parents, or campers swimming in the lake. In the bright sunlight, the people in the photos almost look alive, like I might even know them. I realize I'm thinking like Uncle Lou, seeing worlds within worlds, and that's okay. It helps me feel calm now that I know what it is.

"Look at this one," Ivy says, holding up a photo of a kid and a horse. It's stapled to a map with almost all the letters faded away, except for the words FAR POINT MEADOW. I cough—maybe from the dust, or maybe because I just figured something out.

"Can I see that?" I ask, taking the map from Ivy's hand. "I think I know where Eli went."

57

It's getting later, so we let Aunt Ruthie know that we're heading to the ranch to join the search party. Ivy calls her mom to come and meet us there. We cut through the forest, taking the higher road this time to maybe get a better view of the land, just in case. On one side, the creek runs into the pond where the Stone of Power is. To our left is the long meadow where the black-and-white cows look like chess pieces on a huge green board. Lucky is nowhere to be found.

We walk down the hill from the meadow, the sky darkening into a deep blue. The parking lot at the ranch is full of trucks and cars. Everyone is near the barn entrance. We see Nate there, and Sheriff Hett, who's giving directions to small groups that have gathered around talking about plans and ideas. Jake, the ranch owner, is talking to a larger group by the barn. His little daughter, Perla, walks up to us holding a tray of chocolate chip cookies.

• • • • • •

"What do we do?" I ask.

"I don't know." Ivy shrugs.

Near the barn entrance, Jake lets out a loud whistle that cuts through everyone's talking. He stands next to Eli's dad, his hat in his hands.

"All right, everyone. Thank you to Sheriff Hett and everyone else for coming out. We all know that Levi and his son Eli have had a rough time of it the past year or so. That's why it's even more important that we find Eli by tonight if we can. We don't know much, just that he and Star, also known as the Gray, a four-year-old quarter horse, went missing yesterday—down near old Camp Akiva. Can anyone tell us anything else about what happened or where they might be?"

Ivy looks at me urgently. I shake my head.

"You have to talk about what happened," she whispers. "Tell them what you know, what Boon did? And everything else?"

I shake my head.

"At least show them the map we found? Or tell them what direction you think they went?" I know I should, but I can't find the right words. I think about Aunt Ruthie and what she might say. I think about Eli—that maybe he needs people to speak up for him. Finally, I step forward, but then another voice speaks up.

"It's my fault." Like a ghost, Boon floats into the yellow light of the barn and looks at Eli's dad, and then at the crowd. "We were being stupid, and I was the one who spooked the horse. Eli ran after her." Then he turns to Eli's dad. "I'm so sorry."

Ivy puts her hand on my shoulder and squeezes.

Boon sounds so different, like someone else entirely. Like a kid I would *want* to know.

Eli's dad puts his arm around Boon, and they turn and walk into the barn together, saying words to each other that no one else can hear.

"All right," Jake says. "Please stick with your teams, and message Sheriff Hett with any news."

People break off into their groups. We see Boon stepping up to a big white truck. He looks at us like he might say something, but then he climbs in. Ivy looks at me and shakes her head. "We have to tell them!" She yells out to Boon, but it's too late.

One by one, the cars leave the ranch until it's just me and Ivy. "We can wait until my mom gets here, and then we can go search with them. And why in the world did you not tell them about Far Point Meadow?"

"I don't know," I say. "After Boon spoke up, I got even more nervous. What if I'm wrong? It's just a theory. I've never been there, and I haven't been around here that long. I don't want to lead everyone on a wild-goose chase."

Ivy sighs and turns around. "I'll text them to check Far Point Meadow after they search their own places." I nod.

I see a light, like a candle burning, inside the barn. "Hey, can we do something first?"

Ivy nods. We walk into the barn, but when we get inside, the light is gone. We walk down the long stalls, Flash and Blackberry whinnying and sticking their heads out. Being around them makes me feel brave. Ivy pets each one. She makes cooing noises, like she's talking to a baby.

"Can you speak horse?" I joke. She's not afraid of anything.

"I do now," she says, putting her hand on Misty's muzzle. "Who's the most beautiful horse?"

I make my way to Duke's stall. He is on the other side, where it opens to the outside. His head is hanging over the gate, ears all the way forward, listening into the dark.

"Hi, Duke," I say. His ears roll back. I unhitch the latch to his stall and slowly walk in. I don't have an apple or anything, so I take a handful of hay and lay it out flat in my palm. Duke turns around and steps toward me. He sniffs the hay but doesn't eat any. Instead, he blows a huge breath out of his nose, causing the hay to fly up into my face.

"Duke, you know where Star went, don't you?" He nuzzles my hand, maybe looking for an apple. Then he turns back and moves toward the outside part of the stall again and into the same exact position, ears pointed forward, eyes alert.

"Duke is the best," Ivy says, coming into the stall. "What's he looking at?"

"Probably some raccoons or something out there." I've never seen Duke so alert, though. I wonder if he does know something. Ivy and I stand near him, his body tense.

"What's even over there?" We both look in the direction Duke is looking.

"Cow pastures?" Ivy says. "And then just hills that go on forever all the way toward Far Point Meadow."

"Far Point Meadow! It's out there?"

"Somewhere out there, but it's getting too dark to see, really." Just then we hear footsteps in the barn.

"Ivy?"

"It's my mom!" Ivy says. We pat Duke on the shoulder, but he doesn't move. His body is tight, his eyes fixed in one direction.

"Do you know where Star went, Duke? Did they go to Far Point Meadow?" I whisper to him, then back away and close the latch on the stall.

"Sasha, this is my mom," Ivy says.

I hold out my hand and she shakes it. She looks like Ivy all grown up but without the green in her hair.

"And this is Jennifer." She has a flashlight in one hand and shakes my hand with the other.

"So," Ivy's mom says. "Sasha, it's so nice to meet you. Your aunt and Ivy, of course, have told us so much about you."

"Okay, Mom!" Ivy says, taking her hand. "Can we please start looking?" Her mom and Jennifer both laugh as we make our way to the car. "Should we go to Far Point Meadow first?" Ivy asks.

I don't answer. I stare at the ladder that leads up to the

loft. The light from below softly flickers up, casting shadows high on the ceiling.

"Sasha?" Ivy says. "C'mon."

"Be right there," I say. "I just need to do something." I walk over to the ladder, then slowly climb it, rung by rung, until I count to eighteen. It's much higher up than I thought. I poke my head up through the space where the ladder comes through the floor of the loft. It's darker up here, with just a bit of light making its way up from below. I peer into the loft, and when I do, daylight filters in through a high window, flickering like a candle flame, the light disappearing into the high beams of the barn. I shake my head. Hay bales are piled all around, and a few feet away, the edge of the loft is wide open so the hay can be pushed down easily. On the far side, a few bales are arranged like benches.

"What are you doing?" Ivy has climbed up behind me.

"Looking," I say.

"This is where it happened, right?" Ivy walks over to the edge and looks down. I walk over to the hay bales.

"So much of what's happening now is because of what happened up here," I say.

Ivy looks at me. "Yeah," she says. "I think maybe people needed to listen more." I walk over and sit down on one of the bales of hay.

"I bet Jesse would sit right here and read or do homework. I bet he thought he was so safe. The smell of the barn and the horses, and his brother below." I look back at the opening. I imagine Eli coming through it to check on his brother. I imagine him finding something else. I feel the hair on my arm stand up. A cold wind blows through the barn.

"We better go," Ivy says. We head down quickly, get into their truck, and drive off to search.

58

I've never been part of a search party, but I've seen them on TV and I've played enough video games, so I'm pretty good at problem-solving and finding clues. There's always a quest—and I believe Eli went on some kind of quest to find Star.

"Okay, kids," Ivy's mom says. "Where should we look?"

Ivy looks at me.

I take a deep breath and find the courage to share my theory.

"Eli told me that he and Jesse would sometimes ride to Far Point Meadow. I guess there are long fields there, and streams, and a big waterfall with a swimming hole, and it is really high up so you can see the whole valley. I think maybe Eli went there."

"Wow," Ivy's mom says. "Nice detective work. Even though our service is really spotty, let's text Jake and the sheriff and make sure they know we are checking out Far Point Meadow."

"Can we drive there now?" Ivy asks her mom, who nods

and then puts on some kind of jazz music, the low bass making the car vibrate a little.

"What if Eli caught up to Star and took her out *there* instead of coming back?" I wonder out loud.

"But why wouldn't he come back?" Ivy stares at me. I don't answer for a while. It's a good question. Some horns mix into the jazz now, and the music gets louder. I lean in closer to her.

"If you were him, would *you* want to come back?"

59

We drive slowly, looking out the windows in every direction, but the daylight is almost gone. We reach the bottom
of the hill where Far Point Meadow is supposed to be far
above at the top of the hill. It doesn't seem so far if you
drive. Nothing is.

Ivy's mom tells us it's getting too dark to drive up the
hill. There aren't any roads up to the meadows.

"We don't want to get stuck in some mud, or something
even worse." We get out and look around for as long as we
can, but it's getting hard to see anything. Then Jennifer's
phone buzzes.

"It looks like they're calling it for tonight. The sheriff
says he and Eli's dad will keep searching tonight, and if
anyone else finds anything to let him know. Everyone else
should pick up the search in the morning."

> *The morning*
>> *The morning*
>>> *The morning.*

It seems so far away. I stare out the window and see

lights in the houses—and so much distance between them. In the city, you just look up at any corner anywhere and there's a number or a sign. There's an order to things. It makes sense. Out here, it's just tree to tree, house to house, pond to pond, a different kind of order than in the city.

In the city, even if you're alone, it can be hard to feel it. There's always a car noise, or a screen blaring, or a voice in the apartment upstairs, or something—anything. Everything is a world all by itself. But being alone is different here. It's quiet. I think about Eli out there somewhere, completely alone in the silent dark. I feel it, like something pushing on me from the inside. My heart starts beating faster. The lights in the houses pulse in and out, from bright to dark. Out the window, I see the dark shape of an animal pass through a beam of moonlight between the trees then disappear into the dark.

Ivy holds my hand. "Are you okay?" I feel sleepy. Then, in an instant, the yellow lights of the houses dwindle into gray beneath the fading silver moon. I drift away until I can't hear the music anymore.

60

"Sa . . . Sasha? Are you okay?" I realize that my head is pressed against the window, and it aches. "You fell asleep." I sit up and look around. It feels like it's been a long time, but we are still in the truck.

"Ivy," I say, my voice scratchy, tired. Looking out the window at the quiet night, I feel safe, and I don't want to carry this by myself. I want Ivy to know about what happens to me, even the hard-to-understand parts. "I need to tell you something." Ivy looks at me, then at her mom and asks her to turn up the radio. She scoots closer. "Sometimes," I whisper, "I get really overwhelmed, or anxious."

"Me too!" she blurts out, but quickly quiets down. I slowly tell her about my sensitivities, my anxiety, and even find the courage to talk about the Gray and what it is to me. I try to say it quietly, even though I know her mom and Jennifer might hear me.

"It's this, this kind of fog," I say, "that settles over me—changes the way I see the world—makes everything different. It clouds my vision. Sometimes it feels like I'm in a whole different world that's right next to ours . . ." I get quiet, trying to think of an example. The truck twists and turns through the dark. "You know, like the deer. We see them, they see us, but it almost feels like they are in a different place at the same time. My uncle called it worlds within worlds."

"Okayyy?" She looks confused, but I can see she's trying to understand. I like this most about Ivy. She is such a good thinker. I can trust her with my thoughts, and she always asks great questions. "You mean like day and night?"

"YES!" I say. "Two worlds inside one place! Like the pond where Jumpers lives is one place during the day. Some animals are alive and awake during the day, but at night it comes alive in a different way." She *has to* understand this. But she just looks forward, her mouth open slightly, still thinking.

"Imagine if you could just suddenly walk from daytime into night and then right back again," I explain. "Things are basically the same, but they look different and smell different, and also different creatures come out." She taps her finger on her chin.

"Oh! I know," she says. "You mean like the camp. In one way it's abandoned and dead—old boarded-up buildings, rotting wood. But it's also another place, a whole world alive with memories, but also with the herd of deer, and raccoons, and ghosts like the lost girl, and other spirits?" When she says *spirits*, she sounds like my uncle Lou, like she has no problem saying it. Like it's just normal.

"Yes. Like that, but also, well, also monsters sometimes."

Her jaw drops, like things are coming together. "Monsters? Hmm. Makes sense, I guess. The world is full of monsters, too." She smiles.

"Yeah, it can be scary. It hasn't always been this way, but it got worse after my uncle died. That's when I started calling it the Gray. When I get overwhelmed or anxious, I can feel, like my mom says, the door opening, and I try not to walk through, but it's hard."

"Wait," she says, straining to understand. "The Gray? Like the horse?"

"Right," I say, "just like the horse. Only I didn't even know Eli or Star or anything when I named it that. See what I mean? Worlds within worlds."

She nods and rakes her fingers through her hair. "That sounds really, really hard, Sasha."

"My uncle Lou used to say that I have a gift, that I was sensitive enough to see into the other worlds around us— especially in nature—but it's not really doing us any good right now. It's changed a lot as I've gotten older. Then it got really bad when things got harder at school, and I started spending all my time with computers and video games. It was like spending so much time in those virtual worlds made the walls between this world and the Gray thinner? My doctor back home, he says that I have anxiety attacks. He thinks that's what I mean when I talk about the Gray."

Ivy looks at the light from the car stereo and at the headlights beaming into the forest along the road.

"So this is why you do all that breathing all the time?" she says. "Does it help?"

"Usually, it really does. There are so many different ways to breathe. I used to think breathing was like in . . . and then out . . ." We breathe for a little while together. I show her box breathing.

"I always thought that video games helped my anxiety. Because there are rules in video games. You're safe when you play them, in control—at least, I used to think so. You know, it distracted me, so I didn't have to deal with the real world. It felt that way at first, but after a while, all my time on screens got tangled up with my 'gift' and suddenly I was in the Gray all the time. It got hard for me to tell one world from the other."

Ivy squeezes my hand. We breathe in. We breathe out.

The truck slows down, and the gravelly road feels familiar. We're at Aunt Ruthie's house. I see her at the window.

"We'll find him tomorrow," Ivy says, still holding my hand. "Or maybe the sheriff and Jake will get out there before we do. I know they are checking everywhere as fast as they can—probably searching all night." Her mom and Jennifer nod and smile to show they agree. The kindness in their eyes makes me want to believe them.

I get out of the truck, my legs weak, my stomach churning a little, and make my way down the driveway to the house.

61

"Tell me everything," Aunt Ruthie says as she slides a mug of hot chocolate in front of me. And so I do. I tell her about what happened—every part of it.

"It's okay," she says, and instead of putting on music or doing stuff in the kitchen, she lets us sit in the quiet for a while. But eventually, the silence breaks. "So I had to call your mom, you know."

I nod.

"They're coming."

"They are?" I say, my voice suddenly high-pitched.

"They'll be here the day after tomorrow," she says. Then, she quickly changes the subject. "Maybe we can go by the Stone of Power in the morning!" She says it in the biggest voice she has. But it makes me think of Eli, out there somewhere. Maybe he's all alone.

"What's the point?" I mumble. I feel her hand on my shoulder. "I mean, we call it the Stone of Power, but why? I don't think that rock can do anything. And it certainly didn't give me magic or any power over anything. I never have power—never!" I feel tears coming out.

Aunt Ruthie just sits and listens.

"Are my parents really coming?" I ask, looking up at her.

"They are," she says gravely.

"Does that mean I'm going back?"

Aunt Ruthie takes a long sip of bad-smelling tea. "Maybe?" she says. "Maybe that's up to you."

62

In the morning, I feel even more tired than I did before I went to bed. The sun is shining, but my mood isn't shiny at all. I want to head out right away to Far Point Meadow to look for Eli, but Aunt Ruthie insists we trudge out into the forest and down to the Stone first. At the pond, huge leaves float on the glassy water, and on each there's a tiny frog fresh from tadpole life. They float like a miniature armada in the flecks of sunshine, their silvery-green bodies shimmering.

"Ready?" Aunt Ruthie winks.

She jumps up in one swift motion to surprise them all. Some frogs leap up and off their leaf boats while others slide off, slipping down deep into the water.

Aunt Ruthie laughs. "I love those little guys," she says.

I look for Jumpers. He's nowhere to be found.

We hike over to sit on the mossy flats above the Stone of Power. Aunt Ruthie rests on the edge. I lie down on my stomach and lean over, running my fingers over the face of the Stone and dropping bits of moss into the water.

"I'm scared, Aunt Ruthie. What if Eli doesn't come back?

What if we don't find him? Shouldn't I get going?" I say, letting my frustration leak out.

Aunt Ruthie ignores my questions and says, in her most serious voice, "So, have you thought any more about Uncle Lou's favorite story about Akiva and the Stone?" Frustrated and impatient, I grumble out my answer.

"I've been thinking about it." I hesitate. "And what if I'm getting a little too old for these stories? I'm so tired of magic talk and secret powers. Gift? The Gray? What's the difference? I've never had any power or magic to do anything. Some kind of gift that is." Aunt Ruthie coughs the kind of cough that's on purpose.

"You know the story, then, about how we can't always see it, but little by little, that water is slowly changing the surface of the impossible stone, but what *else* do you know about Akiva?"

"I bet you are going to tell me." I groan, and even though I've been rude, I can't control myself. Then I feel her strong hand on top of my head.

"That's enough," she says firmly. "Now listen. Akiva was different than the others in his community. He didn't talk with too many people. He was kind of an outsider. Different. He had his own struggles. He was poor, and he never really studied the Torah because he couldn't afford to, but he had his own gifts."

"Then he found a stone, right?" I try not to sound sarcastic, but I can't see how this story will help anything right now.

"Yes, well, of course. You knew that part. But what else did he find?"

I feel a sudden but gentle breeze, and when I stare down into the water I can't help but gasp. I see my face rippling in the reflection, but instead of Aunt Ruthie sitting next to me, it looks like Uncle Lou is there. It's murky, but it's *his* face reflected in the water, his long beard and the faded pattern of his checkered shirt. My heart beats faster. I take a breath, and when I exhale, I can even feel his heavy hand on my shoulder, like he's right here with us.

I turn to Aunt Ruthie. "I don't know what else he found. Maybe something that he'd been missing? Or maybe he just saw water taking forever and thought—I need to be patient?"

"*Yes*," Aunt Ruthie says. It's her voice, but also somehow it feels like Uncle Lou is telling the story.

Aunt Ruthie leans closer and hugs me like I just came through her front door after a long time away. "Yes!" she shouts. "You already know the moral of the story: That the water changes the stone little by little. But the *magic* is that when he saw this, the fact that a small trickle of water is able to do *this* to a *stone* allowed him to realize that maybe it wasn't too late for him. Maybe he could work hard and, like the water and the stone, drip by drip, change a little bit at a time, teach himself to be who he wanted to be. He had a special gift to see into the heart of things."

In the water below, the image of Uncle Lou has faded away. Instead two frogs swim to the surface, their eyeballs peering out from their watery world and into mine.

"He went on to be one of the best Torah scholars of his generation. I mean, look, we're still talking about him."

"I know you're trying to teach me something, Aunt Ruthie. But what does this really have to do with me? With right now?"

"Maybe nothing," she says, then pauses with a gleam in her eye. "Or maybe everything."

I sigh, frustrated. "I mean, it's just a story, right? Akiva and his stone—it's not real, right?"

"Are you sure?" Then she grabs my hand and puts it on the face of the Stone.

"Let the water flow over your hand, and then feel along the Stone," she says.

I reach down to where the water is trickling over the surface and pass my fingers over it, feeling its smooth face until I find a shallow groove, like a tiny canyon, the only place where the surface of the stone is different. I leave my fingertip there and watch the water slowly pool and then spill around my finger.

I keep it there for a while, feeling how here, right here in this tiny little place, there *is* a change in something that seemed unchangeable. I get it. But I keep it to myself.

"Aunt Ruthie, do you think Akiva was ever over-whelmed?"

"All the time," she says. "Like all of us. I think once he realized what was possible, he started to become more of who he actually was." When I look at her, I notice she's shaking. Not a lot, but enough for me to notice it.

"Are you okay?" I ask, sitting up. She doesn't respond right away. She looks off toward the trees and then up to the sky and closes her eyes. Aunt Ruthie is always looking out for me. I think of my mom asking me to look out for her, too. Maybe she does need to come back with us to the city. She takes a deep breath, and after she does she opens her eyes to look at me.

"Things are changing for me, too, Sasha. It's okay. It will be okay."

"Aunt Ruthie, you know, it might be fun for you to live with us in the city? And then we could all come out here together whenever we wanted to." She looks back to the sky, her eyes drifting from tree to tree.

"Tell me more, Sasha. What else is on your mind?"

"I thought leaving the city meant that I might be bored, but at least I could leave all the complicated stuff behind. But all that stuff is here, too, only it feels different. Maybe making new friends and being away from the stuff I used to do . . . I don't know. I don't feel *as* lost anymore."

Aunt Ruthie looks at me. The gleam in her eye seems to have grown brighter. "Yes," she says. "Maybe you're a lot like Akiva. The world of who he thought he was supposed to be and the world of who he actually was began to come together because of a stone and some water. Maybe that's what's happening for you?"

"Maybe," I say. "But that's not magic."

She uses her cane to stand up, then lifts it and points it directly at me.

"If the Stone of Power can change, anything can change." She grabs my hand. "Any*one*. How you are in this moment doesn't define you. It's where you go from here that makes the difference." When she says this, I realize something else. All this time, I've been so focused on myself. But it's not just about me—it's about Eli, too.

"Aunt Ruthie," I say. "I have to go find Eli at Far Point Meadow. He *has* to be there. I'm going down to the ranch to find his dad."

Thunder rumbles in the distance through a suddenly graying sky. The forest gets darker from the clouds that have begun to roll in across the sun. There's an earthy smell, like it might rain again. I think of Eli and Star somewhere out there.

Aunt Ruthie leans on her cane in a classic Master Yoda position. "There's something else," she says. "Eli's mom heard what happened. She's coming back to town later today."

I feel my eyes get big.

"And Jesse is coming, too."

63

The ranch is usually busy with Horse Camp and people on trail rides at this time of day, but right now, most everyone is out looking for Eli. I look for Eli's dad, or Jake, but no one I recognize is around. The barn door is open.

I walk in. "Hello?" It looks emptier than I normally see it since some of the horses are out on rides. Flash slowly wanders over to the opening of his stall. I take a sugar cube from a burlap bag and hold it out for him. The rest are silent in their stalls, horse-sleeping. All of them except Duke, who is still standing at the outside section of his stall nibbling on hay. I go into the stall.

"Duke," I whisper. He raises his head slightly. I put my hand on his neck and rub along his shiny brown coat. He bends his head toward me, then he raises it high, his ears going forward. I lean up against him, and when I do, I feel something I've never felt before, a sudden urge to climb up on him and ride.

Ride? Just like I did on Star, but without Eli leading me.

What if *I* took Duke and went to find Eli? I bet Duke

knows the way to Far Point Meadow. But as soon as the thought comes, something else inside me comes up to meet it. I feel my own beating heart, short breaths, my courage slipping away. Duke softly pushes his muzzle into my shoulder, and I feel a little bit braver again. Maybe wanting to find my friend is stronger than my fear.

"Duke, can we do this? What if *we* go look for Star? Maybe it's just like a trail ride?" Duke stands strong, giving me courage. I get the halter, spin it around in my hands, take a deep breath, and slip it around his head. I hook on the lead, and we move out into the area where all the tack is. First, I find the trail maps on the wall and take one. Then I grab a few green apples from the barrel and a few sugar cubes and shove them in my pockets. Next, I try to remember the things I've learned. I find a blanket and swing it over his back. Duke doesn't move, even though he probably knows I'm not very good at this. Then I find a saddle that I think will fit. It's heavy, but I lift it up and onto his back after a few tries. What next? I pull up on the cinch strap then pull it back down. I loop the strap through the saddle ring until it seems tight enough, then I tie a terrible knot. I shake it a little.

Duke moves around a bit—he's used to this process. I don't know if it's tight enough, but it will have to do. I look at the bridles shining on their hooks. He needs a bridle but I've never put one on. I try my best to remember how others have done it.

"Here's the bit, right, Duke?" I take a deep breath.

Duke stands like a rock, lets the bit slide into his huge mouth. I pull the crown over one ear at a time, standing on my tiptoes. I fasten the buckles the best I can. I grab a riding helmet from the wall and fasten it around my chin. When everything is ready, I take one more deep breath and get ready to ride. Right now at least, it looks like everything is in place.

"We can do this, right?" I put my foot into the stirrup, and then, with all my strength, pull myself up as high as I can . . . but it's not high enough. Duke is so tall. I try again and again, hopping up and down, trying to swing myself up, but it's no use.

Then, I get an idea. I pull up the sawhorse where the saddle was and climb on top of it. From this high spot, I get my foot in the stirrup and the rest of me up and over. I land in the saddle. It feels like it should be tighter, but Duke is so big. I can't stop now.

"Thanks for staying so still," I say, then look back. The other horses are awake now. They stare at us, whinnying and bobbing their heads up and down, their mouths open wide. I calm my breathing and open the map I got from the wall. It's an illustrated map, so everything looks like a cartoon and is drawn really big. I find the trail ride from here to Far Point Meadow. It's just through the valley and some foothills along the edge of the forest. On the other side of the meadow is a picture of a waterfall that looks like it's bigger than a mountain.

"Looks easy enough, right, Duke?" I show him the map. "We just go straight for a while, left for a longer while, through some trees, past a waterfall, and we should be there." We slowly step out of the barn. There's no one around. I look out toward the hills.

"Ready?" I gently dig my heel into his side and pull the reins to the right.

64

We cross the low meadow where I rode Duke on that very first trail ride.

"See," I say out loud to no one but Duke. "I did it. I got back on."

The clouds are swirling darker in the sky, and I already feel some drops of summer rain on my skin. We reach a boulder at the end of the meadow. It's a new place where the trail takes a sharp left, winding like an endless snake through miles of high grass. It looked a lot shorter on the map. We ride through the pastures that push against the forest on all sides. Up and down, the rhythm of riding feels like a boat floating in a wide sea.

Cows graze in the field. Some are lying down beneath the beech trees. Aunt Ruthie told me that when cows sit down, it means it's going to rain. She was right. All except Lucky, the giant bull, standing over the others. I blink, and for a moment his horns get longer, his eyes burning in the gray mist, his head lowered. Duke whinnies and raises his head.

When I blink again, Lucky is normal—watchful, ready to charge, but not a monster. I make a clicking noise, because that's what Eli did when he wanted Star to go faster. Then I dig my heel in along with the click. Duke starts to trot, fast. Lucky watches us bounce by. I feel safer, but I have to be careful. I know the Gray is swirling nearby like always, its doors wide open.

We wind along the pastures—past old farmhouses and the biggest trees I've ever seen. All the while, the tiny town is getting smaller and smaller behind us, until it disappears completely. I don't know how long we've been riding, but my behind is numb, my body is wet from the sporadic rain, and my throat aches. I realize we don't have any water. I didn't really bring anything with me. I pull back on the reins, and Duke slows down, eventually letting his head down to graze. I take out the map. The meadow is just a little bit farther. On the cartoon map, the trees look like a giant fence all the way around.

"Well, Duke. It looks like if we keep going for a little while longer, we just have to cross over a stream and go through this tree-fence thing."

We are already so high up. It looks like a place from a fairy tale. Some land that everyone forgot about. My legs have never spent so much time in this position. They are starting to hurt—badly. I know I should get off and stretch.

"I should get down, Duke. Just for a few minutes. But if I do, will you let me get back on?" Duke walks forward, out of the pasture now and into a stand of pine trees. If the map is right, the meadow should be less than a mile from here. I take a deep breath. I better stay on. We are getting close now. Then, I hear thunder in the distance. The drizzle is starting to come down harder. My heart beats faster. It's like a drum pounding inside my head. "Maybe we should go back?"

But Duke doesn't stop or turn around. He walks forward into the trees.

The forest here is thick and overgrown, and the trail gets narrow in places. Duke's body gets tense in the narrow parts.

"Good job," I tell him. We wind in and out of the towering trees glistening in the gradual rain until finally I can see the meadow opening wide in the distance. But there, before the trees end, we see something else standing in the trail. It's a big dog—no, bigger. A coyote. Its limbs are stretched out and low to the ground. It's standing over something, growling, its pointed teeth gleaming.

Then, from the trees, the rest of them come out. More coyotes slink out from behind raspberry bushes, their gray-and-black heads dipped low. I pull on Duke's reins, but he's already stopping. The coyotes silently circle us, holding steady to the trail. The pounding of my heart is louder now in my head. I feel small, and these trees, this place between the sky and the earth, is so enormous. My breath becomes rushed, and my vision starts to get blurry. I feel the Gray on the periphery, but I hold on to Duke. *Be tough—no, be brave*, I think. I feel the rain drenching me all the way to my socks. It's cold. The coyotes break their silence and start to growl. They circle, slinking low toward us, their eyes gleaming in the grayish light, baring their long teeth. Duke tenses. He whinnies at them, loud, and stomps his hooves onto the trail. They come closer, and with every step, I try to find my breath and my voice.

"Duke, I think we need to run." I hold the saddle tight and get ready to kick Duke's side so we can take off, but then, from far away, we hear something—a rumble. Duke's head lifts and his ears go forward. *Boom!* Much closer this time. The trees turn from green to dark gray, twisting overhead in an impossible wind. The coyotes turn their long snouts up. They yip and howl. *BOOM!* More thunder. The rain starts to come down harder. Duke shuffles his front hooves, digging into the muddy trail. Everything seems to change, like I wandered into some wild place where humans aren't allowed. *BOOM!* The hillside rumbles like giants throwing boulders. The trees shake wildly, and the coyotes scatter, black shapes darting into the trees. Duke lifts his head and lets out another high whinny. He raises his front hooves and slams them into the ground, spraying mud everywhere. I hold on to the reins as tight as I can, but the tighter I pull, the higher he raises his head, until it feels like there's no ground beneath us at all. I know Duke is protecting himself, protecting me, but my heart is beating so fast I can't catch it. A lanky coyote bolts in front of us, snapping its giant jaws at Duke. He raises his front legs so high that I start to slide off his back. I drop the lead and grab on to the saddle horn tight with both hands. Duke surges forward suddenly, out into the wide-open meadow. I squeeze the saddle horn with all my might, but it's too late. I'm slipping.

65

When I open my eyes, everything is silvery gray.

66

It feels like I'm standing at the bottom of a shallow bowl with a finger stuck inside my left ear. I try to remember where I am. There's wind on my face, but no basement smell. The pale trees both near and far sway in a quiet wind at the edge of the meadow. My heart beats like it's about to burst. My brain feels cloudy.

I try to remember how to get control. What do I do? Count? Listen? Feel? I feel my hands. They're wet—not with just rain, but with something else, too. They're cut and blood-streaked down the center, a deep rope burn. I was riding—holding the reins. I hold up my empty hands, feel the rain splash onto them.

Everything is louder then quieter then suddenly loud again. I was riding a horse. His name is Duke. I was looking for Far Point Meadow. I breathe. I snap my fingers. Nothing changes. I try to walk, but my legs are so weak from all the riding, and the meadow is so thick with fog that I can barely see anything at all. I'm tired. I need to sit. I was riding a horse. His name is Duke.

Where is Duke? Then, I see my mom's face. I hear her voice. *If ever something serious happens and it feels like you've gone too far in, remember the grounding technique, 5-4-3-2-1. Then just picture a door, walk through, and step back to me.* I take a deep breath. I need to try.

Five things I can see: I look and say them out loud the best I can. "Trees!" I walk toward the trees one tiny step at a time, my hands out in front of me. I'm sweating like I always do when I get this anxious. "Clouds." The clouds swirl in dark delight above me. "A stone." There's a boulder in the middle of the field. "Meadow." I see all the way to the tree line. It looks familiar. But how can it? Have I been here? Maybe in that dream? "Shadows." The coyotes? No. Something else is in the trees, like a swirling gray ghost, moving closer.

Four things I can feel: "Rain." There's rain on my face. On my hands. "Legs." I feel my legs, sore from riding. They feel separate from my body. "Heart." My heart beats loudly in my chest. "Fear." My spine is prickly, hands and feet suddenly cold.

Three sounds I hear: "A voice." It's my dad's voice. I hear it like he's next to me, reading to me before bed. "Howling." A howling in the trees threaded with the wind blowing through the meadow. "Hoofbeats." I hear a thumping, like a quick drumbeat getting louder. Like a herd of wild horses. My chest feels tight.

Two things I can smell: "Latkes" frying in the pan, the

edges crispy. "Horses." The smell of the barn, Flash and Blackberry greeting me, their stalls haven't been cleaned all day.

One thing I can taste: "Cookies." The kind that Daniel's mom makes when we are working on our game.

I close my eyes and take the deepest breath I can. In that thin space, I see Uncle Lou. I hear his voice. *What you are feeling is okay. It's normal to feel things in your guts. It's human. The Gray is part of your world. Use your gift to see. Bring them together.* I start to calm down.

I open my eyes, but when I do, I see something I don't expect. The swirling gray ghost that was coming out of the trees is suddenly here—right above me. I feel vibrations in the air, and some other noise, loud but muffled, like someone screaming underwater. I breathe in. Breathe out. Breathe in. Breathe out. Breathe.

67

"Sasha?" It's more than just a voice. It's someone I know.

He's holding his hand out. I reach for it, and he pulls me up with all his strength.

Eli.

I blink at him for a few moments, his face gray against the gray sky. "Eli, you're in the Gray?"

"The what?" he says, looking around. He waves his hand, and things start to change.

Behind him, the sky slowly brightens to blue. The swirling clouds melt into fluttery wisps. The trees burst into deep green through the thinning fog. He pulls me all the way up with one hand, and in the other hand are reins holding Star, who is grazing just behind him without a saddle.

"You're okay, Sasha, at least I think you are. You're breathing heavily. But you're okay. I found you." He helps me lean against a boulder.

"Found . . . found *me*?" Above me the clouds are bright white. "But I was looking for *you*." I feel my insides swirling.

"Well, I guess we found each other, then." He puts his

hand on my shoulder, then takes off his backpack and hands me his water bottle and a granola bar.

I drink deeply and gobble the whole thing down. Everything's coming back to its right color, and sunlight is now pouring through the clouds, turning the meadow gold.

"Duke!" I suddenly remember. "I rode Duke all the way out here. I thought you might be here. But then there was thunder, and coyotes—a whole pack of them. We have to find him."

"I *think* he's fine." Eli points down the slope of the meadow where it runs along a river. Duke is there, grazing on clover, his brown coat shining in the sun and his saddle missing. "He was right here all along, looking out for you."

"Duke!" I shout. He looks up for a moment, turns his ears toward me, sighs, and then goes back to grazing.

"Eli. What happened?"

68

"Rest for a second." Eli motions for me to lean against a rock. He pours some water over the cuts on my hands.

"I knew you would come here," I say again, coughing a bit, my stomach turning over and twisting into knots. Eli looks over at Star.

"When Star took off like that, I just felt, well—it's like nothing else mattered. I couldn't lose her, too. I didn't want to make the same mistake again," Eli says softly.

"What mistake?"

"Of letting her go without me trying to stop her."

I look at him. His eyes are far away.

"So, you followed her into the woods?"

Eli kneels down. Even kneeling, he's taller than I am. "I also ran away for another reason," he says.

I gulp down some more water.

"I know you think I'm brave, Sasha, but I'm not. The fighting didn't hurt, but when they went after Star, it felt like my heart was going to burst out of me. Everything got blurry—I thought I might start crying. And I could *not* let them see that."

"So you ran?"

"I ran." He sighs and drops his head a little. I try to think of something to say, but he continues. "It's just that I didn't want to fail Star like I failed Jesse. I can't stop wishing I had done something sooner to help my brother, so I took off after Star. I didn't want it to happen again." I've never heard Eli talk this much, almost like he's a different version of himself. Hearing his words, I think about how much I wished the opposite with Jeremy. I wished I *hadn't* acted, or whatever it might take to erase the memory of what I did to him. There must be something in the middle that's the right thing.

"But I'm sorry, Sasha. When I ran like that, I blew it. I was supposed to be there for you, too, and I failed you."

"Where did you run to?"

Eli points toward the forest.

"I tried to follow her trail. But the more I ran, the harder it got to see or hear anything. When I got to the trees I looked back, and it was the weirdest thing . . . the trees looked like shadows, and I couldn't see anyone or hear anything. My heart was beating so fast, and I just ran until I had to stop and rest."

Was Eli in the Gray, too? I want to ask so many questions, tell him that I understand what he's talking about, but I wait because Eli starts talking again.

"After that, I took off, deeper into parts of the forest behind the camp, looking for Star. But the trees were all twisted up, overgrown, hard to even see where the branches of one tree ended and another began. That's when . . ."

"What?" I say, sitting up.

"Well, I saw something. I thought it was a horse, so I ran toward it, but it was just some raccoons climbing up a tree. But when I looked down, I found her trail, fresh hoofprints in the mud."

"So you just followed her hoofprints all the way here?" I ask.

"Most of the horses at the ranch have known these trails by sight and smell since they were young, so I thought she must be somewhere out here."

I try to calm down. "I remember you talking about Jesse, and Far Point Meadow, and the waterfall. I thought you might try to come here!"

"Good guess. I can't believe you rode out here on your own. Maybe *you* should be *my* bodyguard."

We smile at each other.

"So, I hiked up here," he says, "and I found Star standing in the trees trying to keep from getting wet. She was definitely glad to see me—even though she'd never admit it."

"So, you just stayed here?"

"Yeah. I wasn't ready to go back, and I know these woods really well, so I just camped out in some secret spots."

I try to imagine camping on my own in the forest.

"But then this morning I was getting ready to come back. I knew people"—he points at me—"would be getting worried. My dad's had it hard enough. Anyway, I was riding out, and then I saw something really strange, so we rode as fast as we could. It was you, crawling through the meadow like you were blind or something."

"I could see you, too," I say.

"I hope so—I mean, I'm pretty big for my age."

"No, I mean . . . well . . . sometimes when I panic or get too anxious, it gets out of control." I stop. I don't know how to explain it to him without sounding ridiculous, but then he jumps in.

"You feel like you are in another place but it's also the same? Like you can't see or even breathe sometimes?"

"Yeah," I say. "Like everything is a shadowy fog."

He nods, then looks me straight in the eye so I know he understands.

"Do you ever see things? Animals? Monsters? Ghosts?" I ask him.

He looks at me strangely, then nods. "I, I didn't think any of that was real," he says. "I've always felt weird things like this, ever since I was little. Jesse is the only person I talk to about it. Well, and the horses. I always feel safe with the horses. That's why I like spending so much time at the ranch. But things changed after Jesse left. I felt cut off from that, like I couldn't feel anything anymore." He gets silent for a while. "When I saw you in the meadow today," Eli says, "it made me think about the other times you were like this. Like at the old boathouse when Boon was going to knock you out. I could tell you were out of it, but somehow Boon bugged you enough that you tried to come back—then you got sick all over him, which I liked."

We sit in the sun. Eli wraps a bandanna around my right hand.

After a while, when my stomach isn't somersaulting over itself anymore, we walk slowly down to where Duke is grazing near the beech trees. He lifts his head and puts his muzzle into my shoulder.

"Thanks for looking out for me, Duke," I say.

Eli takes Star's bridle and loosely wraps the reins around a low tree limb. Then he does the same for Duke—secure, but loose enough that both horses can enjoy the clover that's growing everywhere.

"C'mon. Let me show you something." We walk into the forest, where the leaves are still wet and everything smells like damp soil. Up ahead, we hear the deep whoosh of water, and then we see it, the river spilling out of a wide pond, and at the other end, a waterfall crashing onto the rocks below, water spraying up and foaming into the pool.

"Is this where you camped out?" I ask. Eli nods.

"This is our place," he whispers. "Where me and Jesse would ride to after all the work was done for the day."

"This is so cool," I say.

"I think this is really why Jesse wanted to hang out with me at work. He loved riding here."

"What's that?" I point to a dark spot near a huge boulder just behind the spot where the water is falling the hardest.

"That's the secret spot. It's a small cave just behind the waterfall. You can actually fit inside it. You'd think it would be so loud, but it's quiet in there. Peaceful. Jesse loved going there more than anywhere else. If anyone has a gift, it's him. He used to say that the meadow and the woods were full of forest spirits. He used to wait for one he called the King, a huge stag with shining blue eyes."

Eli stops and walks closer to the water. He picks up a flat stone and skips it across the surface. Three skips. I look around to find a stone of my own. I pick it up. I try to skip it, but it makes one big *plop*.

"When everything happened . . . well . . . it's like the world just blew up," Eli says. "Our parents were arguing all the time. My dad just worked and worked. It was all he could do. He still does. But Jesse had it the worst. He didn't like that everyone was blaming me—saying that I lost control."

"One day, Jesse disappeared. The whole town went looking for him, but I knew where he was." Eli points to the cave entrance. "When I found him, he had a backpack full of juice boxes, a pack of string cheese, and his Ninja Turtle blanket. He used to say that this place was pure magic. That this cave behind the waterfall was a portal, and that it could take us to any other place we wished to go."

"Like maybe to the secret tunnel behind the Stone of Power?"

"Yes," Eli laughs. "Exactly!"

"I didn't know he ran away," I say.

"Yeah. I think after that, my mom and dad decided it was just too much. The woods and the waterfall couldn't cure him, even though me and Jesse thought it could. That's when they left."

I want to tell him, more than anything, that his mom and Jesse are coming *today*. I try to breathe, to find the courage to tell him, but I just can't. What if it's too much for him to handle? What if he gets overwhelmed and rides off again?

"You know the whole town is looking for you?"

Eli side-eyes me.

"Looking for me? Nobody's looking for me, Sasha."

I look back through the trees to where Duke and Star were chomping on the clover, but their heads are raised, their ears rolled forward. Then we hear voices shouting from somewhere in the trees.

69

We rush back to where the horses are. And there, on the far side of the meadow, we see a group of people coming toward us. They are all wearing big backpacks, and there are two dogs barking wildly on long leashes. When they see us, they start running.

Eli grabs Star's reins like he might just jump up and ride away. But then a voice, clear as the morning, calls out.

"Sasha!" It's Ivy, her long hair flying everywhere as she bolts through the meadow, and next to her is Ally, her eyes hidden behind her mirrored sunglasses, her hands being yanked around by a big white dog. Johnny and Oscar carry giant walking sticks, and there, just behind them, we see Boon, his bright blond hair shining in the sunlight.

"Sasha! Eli! We found you. I can't believe it!" Ivy yells.

Eli looks at me, then tightens his grip on the reins, eyes squinting.

"I can't believe you brought them here," he grunts.

"He didn't," Ivy says. "We came out here last night, but it got too late." Johnny takes a water bottle out of his back-pack and holds it up for Eli. Eli shakes his head.

"When the sheriff told us you might be out here, we volunteered to come." Johnny opens the water and takes a drink. Oscar sets his backpack down on the ground with a thud. Ally puts her hand to her face and takes off her mirrored sunglasses for the first time ever. I am surprised to see she has bright green eyes that actually look kind.

"All of you volunteered?" I say, staring at Boon.

"Even him," Ally says.

Eli takes a step back. He settles Star's bridle just right and puts his hands on her back like he's ready to jump on.

"Wait," Boon shouts.

I feel my breath start to shift. My body tightens.

"Look, Eli. I . . ."

Eli stops, but then he slowly turns, attaches the bridle to a tree branch, and balls his fists.

But Boon already has his hands up. "Hey, c'mon. I didn't come out here to fight you again." Eli steps forward.

"Then why did you come?" Eli gets closer. I feel the anger like electricity in the air.

"I don't know," Boon says, looking down at the ground. His friends look at him, their heads all tilted to the side.

"Yes, you do," Ally says, looking straight at Boon. "You and Eli were best friends, and then weirdness happened. It's okay to say you miss him."

Boon looks up. "It's true, all right? When everything happened—I knew you were just trying to take care of Jesse."

I see Eli's body get even more tense.

Boon takes a step back.

Eli doesn't say anything. His face slips into the Eli I first met, his mouth a thin line across his face, his eyes drifting down.

Duke nudges my shoulder, whinnies low.

"Then why are you so mean all the time?" I shout.

They all look down or away—all except for Boon, whose eyes are fixed on Eli.

"You just stopped talking to me," Boon says to Eli. "You stopped playing baseball. You ignored me when I called or came over."

Eli's face relaxes. He looks at Boon, still silent.

"I tried to help you, but you just disappeared," Boon says.

Ivy walks over to Duke and pets his neck just below his mane.

"Your dad's waiting for you back at the ranch. He's been worried."

Eli's shoulders fall. I can see his eyes welling up with tears.

"How?" Eli says, breaking his silence, his voice hoarse. He looks down. I can see him shaking. I start to walk over, but Boon is already there. He says something to Eli, barely loud enough, and then he steps forward and puts his hand out. A strong breeze flows through the meadow. They shake hands for a long time.

Ally smiles and puts her sunglasses back on. "Finally."

Boon and Eli talk, and the rest of us feel the relief of it, too.

"Look!" Ivy says, grabbing my hand. Across the meadow, a herd of deer moves silently through the forest. In the center, a huge stag with tree-branch antlers steps out into the meadow and watches us, its blue eyes shining brightly through the sunlit morning.

70

"Those are the ancient deer," Ivy whispers.

I hold Duke's lead a little tighter. "How do you know?"

"Did you see that stag? Most of the deer near the camp and around town, they're younger, more used to people. But that stag? He's one of the ancient ones. It's like another world up here, you know?"

I do. I know all about other worlds.

"Speaking of other worlds . . ." She points down the hill where Eli is walking, leading Star on one side and Boon on the other. "I wonder what they're talking about."

"He's probably begging him to get back on the baseball team," Johnny interrupts.

Far Point Meadow is behind us now. I imagine that I can still hear the waterfall. Down the hill, I see a dirt road, a few trucks, and Jake in his bright blue shirt. When he sees us, he waves, calls out to us, and throws his hat into the air in celebration.

Ivy puts her head on my shoulder and whispers, "Does Eli know that Jesse's coming back today?"

"How could he? I mean, I didn't tell him. Should I tell him?" I stop, and Duke almost runs me over.

"I don't know—I mean, wouldn't you want to know?"

But then she pushes me playfully in the shoulder and changes the subject. "Hey," she says. "Do you realize you did it? You actually rode out here *on* Duke, *by* yourself, and found them."

I look over at Eli. His boots are caked with mud; his steps heavy from all the time spent out here—but he's smiling. He reaches into his coat pocket, pulls out an apple, and feeds it to Star.

"Actually, Ivy, Eli found *me*," I say.

Ivy flips her hair. "What?"

"Yeah, I rode all the way. It was a little scary, but I felt really good riding Duke, and he took care of me, but then there were these monster coyotes, and crazy thunder, and Duke got spooked. It was too much for both of us, and the next thing I knew I was in the Gray."

Ivy looks at me, then puts her hand in mine and squeezes hard.

"I have a question for you. That day, that first day, in the boathouse with Boon, when you got sick? Is that what happened to you?"

"Yes! And then I threw up on him because that happens, too, sometimes."

Ivy laughs. Then she looks at me with the eyes of someone who would never let me down. "Thanks for telling me about that, Sasha—about all of it. But you know, you don't seem that anxious *or* overwhelmed to me. Isn't it kind of normal for everyone to feel that way sometimes? I think you're the toughest kid I know." She punches me in the arm, and before I get a chance to tell her that I think things might really be changing, she laughs out loud and starts dancing in the meadow—spinning gracefully beneath the sky.

71

When we get to the road, everyone is shaking hands and putting out water buckets for the horses. Eli convinces me that we should ride back now that the day is bright.

Everyone agrees, but they ask us to ride along the dirt roads so they can keep track of us and make sure we get back safe.

Jake hands me a fresh blanket to put on Duke's back and helps me refasten the saddle. Then he hands me some sugar cubes. I feed them to Duke, palm flat, and he swipes them up with his tongue.

"Okay, Duke," I say cautiously. "Time for me to get back on, okay?" Duke stands like a statue. I dig my toe into the stirrup and heave myself up and over the saddle. It's not graceful—my legs are so sore they feel like they might fall off—but I make it.

"Are you going to make those groaning noises the whole time?" Eli sneers while we ride.

"Sorry," I say. "My legs are really sore." We ride around the base of the hills, the trees rising and falling like waves over the green meadows.

"So, you and Boon are friends again?" I say, not looking over at him.

Eli doesn't say anything for a long time.

"Yeah," he says. "I guess so."

The road winds down and we come to a stream where both horses take a long, deep drink.

"So," I mumble. "Does this mean I don't need a bodyguard anymore?"

Eli looks over, his mouth a straight line stretched across his face.

"Oh, I don't know. I mean, me and him are friends again, but I don't know about *you* and him."

I feel my stomach start to hurt, and my heart beat a little faster. Then Eli's mouth curves up into a smile. "C'mon! It's a joke. But yeah, you don't need a bodyguard anymore. Besides, you never paid me."

"I tried to a few times," I say, but I can tell he's not being serious.

"It's okay," he says. "Let's just call it even."

I start to think about all of our time together, and all the ways Eli has helped me. And maybe how I've helped him. We understand each other.

"But listen," Eli says, "just be careful around Boon. I still don't completely trust him—and we both know that he can be the meanest kid in town, even if he is starting to come around."

I look over at him again because for a moment I think he's mad, but then he starts smiling. I smile, too, but I know I have to tell him about his mom and Jesse before we get back.

72

By the time we reach the final hill, my legs are numb, but there is still a long, straight stretch to go. We can see the ranch at last, down at the end of the long dirt road, and everyone is already there waiting for us. Even from this far away we can see the parking lot full of cars and trucks and people.

"What the?" Eli mutters. Then he spits into the dirt.

"That's a lot of people," I say.

Eli pulls back on Star's reins. "I don't know, Sasha. I don't think I . . ." Then he raises the reins, turns Star in the other direction, and clicks twice in his cheek.

"Wait!" I shout, trying to turn Duke, but he's like a giant barge. "Duke, turn—please turn. Come on."

When I finally get him turned around, Star is already trotting away with Eli. I yell, "Stop!"

They don't stop.

"You can't run away!"

Nothing.

Then, from deep down, I try the bravest thing I can think of.

"Jesse's there," I say.

Star stops. Eli slowly turns her around and they walk back toward us.

His face is bright red, his eyes narrow. "What are you talking about?"

"I didn't know how to tell you, but they said that your mom and . . . and Jesse were coming back. I guess when you disappeared, your dad called them."

For a moment, his red face turns pale. I can see his breaths getting faster—his chest rising and falling faster than it's supposed to, his eyes lost into the hills far away. I catch up to him. He drops the reins, and I see his shoulders slump a little.

"Eli!" I shout.

Star snorts, lifting her front hooves, then pounding the ground a bit. Eli opens his eyes and shakes his head, his breathing still fast. He holds tight to the saddle horn, his chest going in and out. I ride closer.

"Breathe in through your nose—one, two—and out through your mouth—one, two. Inhale, one, two . . . and exhale one, two."

Duke and Star stay still, side by side, letting us breathe, lending us their steadiness. I can see the color in his face changing back to normal.

"Thanks," he whispers.

Then he pulls up the reins and looks down the road toward the ranch. I can see his eyes are wet. And then, suddenly, his giant frame slumps over, his head in his hands, and he's sobbing. Usually I'm the one who cries, but I know enough to just let him cry and not try to say anything. When he's ready, he wipes his face on his sleeve. I turn Duke around, and we ride together, hoofbeat by hoofbeat, back to the ranch in sweet silence.

73

Aunt Ruthie looks like Master Yoda at the Jedi council, so short in the huge crowd of people but impossible to miss. When she sees me, she runs over and practically picks me up. "You mensch!" It feels like the whole town is here. Even though I don't know that many people, I see Johnny, Oscar, and Boon talking to other grown-ups, and Nate is here with some of his Krav Maga students. The owner of the diner, the small freckle-faced girl, and so many others—everyone putting all their troubles and problems aside to help each other make things right.

"How was your ride?" Ivy asks, walking over.

"I was scared to tell him about Jesse. I thought maybe it would be too much. He was nervous anyway when he saw everyone, but I don't think he would have come back if I hadn't told him."

"I'm glad you did. Look." She points over the top of the crowd to a spot near the entrance of the barn.

Aunt Ruthie grabs my hand. Not for me, but for what we see.

Eli and Star are there, and a woman, tall like Eli, has

her arms wrapped around him, his face buried in her dark curly hair. Next to her is a little boy with long blond hair wearing jeans and a striped shirt. Eli kneels down so he's face-to-face with the boy. He puts his hand on top of the boy's head and says something. They laugh. Then Eli picks the boy up and spins him around, his legs flailing in the air. Then, all at once, he swings the boy up and onto Star, who stays incredibly still. The little boy leans forward, closing his eyes and wrapping his arms around Star's neck the best he can.

A little later, when we walk over to where they are, Eli puts his hand on my shoulder. "Sasha, this is my mom," he says. "And this guy on top of Star, this is Jesse."

74

When I wake up the next morning, Aunt Ruthie is standing in the doorway.

I rub my eyes.

"Good morning," she says, holding my medicine in one hand and a glass of water in the other. "Don't forget."

"Sorry," I say. "I got distracted."

She sits down on the bed. "A lot has happened. How do you feel?" she asks.

"Happy to be in this warm bed. And . . . ugh, my legs are so sore from riding."

"Well, how about one more little walk to the Stone before your parents get here later?"

My parents. That's right. I feel a knot in my stomach. It's not that I don't want to see them, but so much has happened. I feel like I'm just getting started here.

"Do you think they'll take me back with them?"

Suddenly, I can smell my room back home. I feel the concrete of the city streets under my shoes. My mind fills with thoughts of home: hot dog carts, computer screens, video games. I hear the clicks in my brain, feel the mouse in my hand. I think of Daniel, but then also of Jeremy. I start to shake a little. Aunt Ruthie puts her hand over mine. Then I start to think about how life here is a lot like life there. So many issues and difficult stories: Uncle Lou, the camp closing, Ivy's mom not wanting her to ever go to the city, everything that happened to Eli and his family. Life is complicated everywhere.

"Do you *want* to go back with them?" I don't answer.

Aunt Ruthie reaches deep into her pockets and pulls out Uncle Lou's tiny dragon carving. She squeezes it, then puts it in my hand. "He would want you to have this." I hold the treasure tight, imagining it in his hand not so long ago.

"Do you think I've changed enough?"

Aunt Ruthie looks like she's trying to hold a smile inside her face.

"Why don't we talk it over by the Stone?"

We walk through the forest. The sun is bright in the morning sky, and the air is getting warmer. We hear the frogs croaking, but this time Aunt Ruthie ignores them and just walks straight to the Stone of Power. We sit down on the moss.

"These have been some incredible days," she says, raising her hands into the air like she's reaching for the leaves. I get myself ready for another long story, but it doesn't come.

We listen to the frogs, to the wind in the leaves, my

breath flowing easily in and out. I stretch out on the moss and lean over so I can see my reflection in the pond below. I find the trickle of water over the Stone and trace the groove along its face.

"Is it any deeper?" Aunt Ruthie asks, leaning over to see it, too.

"I can definitely feel it, but I'm not sure it's any deeper."

Aunt Ruthie stretches her arm over the edge to feel for it, too.

"Not yet," she says. "Not yet. But little by little, even this rock will change form. Little by little. It's magic, Sasha."

"It's water, Aunt Ruthie. It's just ordinary water."

"Isn't that what magic is?" She sits up. "Isn't magic just ordinary things being extraordinary?"

At first this feels like a typical Aunt Ruthie thing to say. But then I look up.

"You mean like the water slowly changing the rock?"

"Yes," she says. "Like worlds inside of us coming together or a friendship slowly changing the friends inside of it."

She places her hand on the face of the Stone. "You need to remember the story of the stone and the water. You can remember that change happens, little by little, in even the most immovable places. That's the key to the story. That's the magic you need."

I feel the water on the Stone. I stare at my reflection in the water.

"I think I've changed, Aunt Ruthie."

She starts to get up, leaning on her cane, but I can tell that, even as strong as she is, it's getting harder for her. "Use the Force, Aunt Ruthie," I say, but she doesn't look amused. I get up and help her.

"Your father loves you. Just remember that. Have you changed enough for *you*? That's all that matters."

75

My father looks different. Instead of his usual work clothes, he's wearing a faded Camp Akiva T-shirt and jeans. He's standing next to a small, one-step bridge over a dripping stream and staring at a wooden gnome inside a hollowed-out tree stump. When he sees us, he smiles wide and gives me and Aunt Ruthie a huge hug.

"All right," she says, grabbing his face and squeezing his cheeks way too hard.

When she finally lets go, he puts his hand on my head. "Sasha, look at you. You've been out in the sun? Your hair is even lighter!"

I look at my arm. I guess I didn't think about that. Then he kneels down in front of me. His beard is longer.

"Hi, Dad." Then I let myself fall forward. He lets me crash into him, his huge arms all the way around me.

"I've missed you, Sasha. We've been hearing all about what's been going on. We came as soon as we could."

"I'm okay, Dad. I am." He leans back and looks at me.

"Is it true you were riding horses?" He smiles wide.

I nod. "Yes, his name is Duke. You have to meet him!"

He laughs and then holds both my hands. "I can't wait." We walk over to the bridge. My dad looks it over, carefully inspecting—and admiring—its construction. "Have you been taking your medicine? You know, practicing your breathing and all that?" He stumbles over the words. He doesn't like to say any of it, but I can tell he's trying. He kneels down, shaking one of the loose planks on the bridge. "Did you, you know—have any episodes?"

Episodes.

"Yes," I mumble. "I had a lot."

"You did?" I can hear it then, the same exasperation in his voice, circling above me like a heavy cloud of questions waiting to be asked.

"Yes, but it's okay, Dad. Because for every time I went into the Gray, I learned more about it, and about me. It's part of who I am. Maybe a gift, maybe not. And I'm learning to feel more grounded."

"Yes," he says. "The Gray. Right."

"I know you don't like when I talk about it. But I know a lot more now. I feel more like myself. And all these things I deal with? I am not alone."

I see him wanting to ask more questions, but I continue, "I just need to keep working on it."

He nods, desperately trying to hold it all in. Then he points at the carving of the coyote near the end of the house.

"Uncle Lou carved that," he says. "When you were little, you would spend hours searching all around the property, all the way to the stream, because Uncle Lou carved all these animals and gnomes, and even built these bridges everywhere. You used to say that they were alive, that you were tired from chasing them everywhere. I thought it was adorable. Then when you got older, you started to tell us that they were chasing you. Remember that?" I laugh a little because I remember it all. "But after a while, everything got so real for you. I didn't always know how to take it. How to help you."

"I know," I say quietly.

"He was like you—you know? He believed that these different worlds are all happening at the same time and sometimes crash into each other. I used to get confused. I didn't understand him. But Sasha? Whatever this all is, I am here. I'm sorry for not always understanding. I promise to do the best I can." He grabs me in another bear hug, and I don't want to let go.

From the house, we hear the screen door creak open. "Sasha!" Mom runs over and squeezes me so hard my back cracks. She lifts me up. "Are you all right? Tell me everything. I brought bagels—come inside. You can tell us all about your adventures. Aunt Ruthie has been filling us in."

76

Later that day, we all get cotton candy ice cream at the diner—two scoops. And I take my parents to meet Nate.

"Sasha's an animal. He's learning so much." He swings a slow, wide blow, and I lean forward to block it with the outside of my hand, then counterstrike. My dad nods, and Nate talks to him about Krav Maga and jujitsu, and everything else.

I walk outside to where my mom is standing with Aunt Ruthie. Across the street, in the park, I see the place where Boon and I got in a fight. Mom points to the crowd of kids by the baseball field.

"Oh, did you get to play baseball, Sasha?" Dad asks.

Aunt Ruthie side-eyes me. I see Boon is up to bat. I hear the crack of the bat as he hits one really deep.

I look for Eli, but he isn't there.

"I didn't. We did lots of other things, though."

Mom holds my hand, gently squeezing it like she does every time she has to tell me something, or when she's worried about me—which is a lot of the time. We walk across the street to the bench in the park and sit down.

"Sasha, your dad and I, and Aunt Ruthie—we think you've been doing really well here. We know that you want to get back home, and see your friends, and everything else . . ." She's squeezing my hand so hard it actually hurts a little.

"But we want you to stay for a few more weeks . . ." She trails off, like "a few more weeks" is not a set time. "Actually, all of us will stay with Aunt Ruthie. We think we all need some time away. Some time together."

"Cool," I say, slowly taking this all in. I feel my breath getting faster, my heart pounding a little harder in my chest, but not because I'm anxious. I'm something else? Happy. I'm happy in a way I didn't expect.

"Really?" she says, lightening her grip on my hand.

I nod.

"That's wonderful." She leans in to hug me.

My breathing calms down.

"I can't wait to hear about *all* of your adventures."

● ● ● ● ● ●

Before we get in the truck, my phone dings. It's a text from Daniel. It's a picture actually—a black-and-white image of a squirrel holding an acorn. Behind it is a huge oak tree, and behind that is a giant building soaring into the sky. It looks like art. *When are you getting back? I really got into photography this summer—I have millions of photos to show you. I didn't do much with our game. Maybe when you get back?*

Awesome photo, I write back. *See you next month.*

77

Aunt Ruthie teaches Ivy and me how to braid challah. Mine could use improvement, but Ivy's looks like tiny intertwining snakes, too small to be loaves of bread.

"How did you get them so small?" I ask.

"I DON'T KNOW, OKAY?" She slams her hand down on both "snakes," laughing and crying at the same time. "It's too sticky! I don't get it!" Her mom walks over and nods.

Aunt Ruthie puts her giant spoon down and wipes her hands on her apron. "Here, you just need a little more egg wash." She winks at me. She's always doing this. Winking or looking at me funny, like we're pulling off some prank, or are part of a secret plan.

Ivy's mom and Jennifer chop vegetables in the kitchen with Mom while Dad loads up the red wagon with blankets, drinks, silverware, and a bunch of other boxes. Aunt Ruthie brings two wooden candleholders—they've been carved into trees with arms holding up the place where the candles go.

"Don't forget these. It will be nice having Shabbat all together outside now that the sun is going down later."

"It won't be sundown, though," Dad says.

"Well, we don't have to light them, but they were your uncle's favorite. Besides, this will be the first Shabbat we've observed in a long time."

Dad keeps loading the red wagon until it's overflowing.

While we wait for the challah to finish baking, Aunt Ruthie hooks her arm through mine.

"Thank you, Sasha, for making this a summer to remember." I smile.

"It's not over yet—I mean, we get to stay even longer now," I answer brightly.

"And there's even more," she says. I'm confused, and then I get a little nervous. "I'm coming back with you," she whispers. "Whatever you did seems to have worked." I let out a breath. I can't believe it. I start to think of Aunt Ruthie in our apartment, walking down our block. But then my eyes wander all around the house, at the small carved statues, the walking sticks, the paintings on the walls. Aunt Ruthie must see me looking because that's when she leans in.

"Oh, don't worry, we aren't giving up this place—the house, the pond, the Stone. Oh no. We will come to visit all the time." She hugs me tight, then suddenly yells in a voice loud enough for everyone to hear.

"All right, before we go, Ivy and I have a little performance for you. She's been working very hard."

We clear away the coffee table. Aunt Ruthie puts on the music, and they step into the center of the living room. The music fades in then booms and breaks. Aunt Ruthie and Ivy swing their legs, turn their shoulders—they are ageless, floating. It feels like a theater inside her little house, yet another world inside a world.

After the performance the house erupts in loud applause and shouts for an encore until Ivy puts on some funky music, and she and Aunt Ruthie pull everyone into the center of the room for a dance party.

So many things make me nervous, including dancing. But there's something about the beat of the music and the warmth of the whole family in here together that helps me be brave. Ivy pulls me in with one hand and swings me around. That's when I think of it.

"Ivy!" I shout. She slows down a bit for my sake. "So, will you come visit us in the city this fall? I could show you around?" She stops dancing for a second, then pulls me in tightly because her mom is dancing right next to us, her eyes suddenly stern.

"Please, Mom?" Her mom looks around the room, then takes a deep breath and rolls her eyes.

"Isabel," she says firmly, Ivy's real name echoing through the room for everyone to hear. Ivy holds her breath, but then her mom breaks into a smile. "How can I hold you back," she says. "I guess we'll just have to take you to the city." Ivy leaps into a hug with her mom, then turns to me.

"Will you show me Central Park?" she asks me.

"And Julliard?" I say. She smiles widely, then grabs my hands and starts jumping up and down. We move our bodies to the music until the challah comes out of the oven.

78

The hike through the woods is slower with all of us and the red wagon full of food.

"Do you think we'll see Jumpers?" Ivy asks. But it's late afternoon, and by the time we get there, the frogs are everywhere, zapping gnats and flies with their tongues.

"Jumpers!" Ivy rushes toward the banks of the water.

Aunt Ruthie leans over and whispers, "She's worse than me."

We spread out blankets near the mossy ridge above the Stone of Power, then set out the candlesticks, plates of challah, and bowls and dishes filled with everything good. Down by the water, Ivy stares into the eyes of a frog half-way submerged in the water, its lamp-like eyes locked with hers.

Then from the other direction, we see four figures emerge from the forest trail, and there is nothing ghostly about them. Eli's in the lead, dressed in an untucked button-down shirt. His mom and dad walk just behind him, and in between them, holding their hands, is Jesse, his hair awkwardly combed. He walks shyly with his mom.

"Well, if it isn't the ghost," Aunt Ruthie says. She smiles at Eli, then lightly pats his cheek.

Mom pours everyone something to drink, and we try to be polite with each other until finally Aunt Ruthie tells us to cut it out and go play for a while.

I look at Jesse. "Hey, Jesse. Do you like frogs?"

He nods.

I run down to where Ivy is, and by now there are seven frogs staring at her, their eyes sticking just out of the water.

"It's Jumpers," she says. "Jumpers is calling them."

We lie down next to her, quietly.

"Don't say anything. Try to talk to the frogs with your mind."

I look over at Jesse, and he looks at me, and then we can't help it. We start laughing, and we can't stop. We try to catch frogs, but mostly we catch mud on our clothes—except Jesse, who catches a skinny green one.

"Nice catch," I say. "What are you going to name him?"

He shrugs, then looks at the frog in his hands. He lowers his hands down to the water and opens them. The frog leaps into the water with a deep *plop*.

"C'mon," Aunt Ruthie calls out. "Time to eat!"

We start to head up the hill, but Jesse is still staring straight at the Stone of Power.

"I remember this rock." He says it so quietly I almost don't hear him.

"That's the Stone of Power," I say, turning back to him.

"You know, some people say that it's actually a gateway to secret tunnels that lead to other secret places all over this valley."

"Really?" he says.

"Well," I say, "what do you think?" We look at the Stone together, and for the first time, I think I see its real power. The Stone can stand in all worlds at once. It's mysterious, out of place, misunderstood, and hard to understand—just like all of us are, and that's okay. It's just like that sometimes, and it doesn't mean we aren't strong—we are strong and also changing a little at a time.

● ● ● ● ● ●

Later, we sit on the blankets and eat, talking and laughing together, the afternoon sun shining through the trees. Eli looks really different when he's not dirt-covered and wearing his big green jacket or floating through the Gray. He looks like a kid.

After we eat, Aunt Ruthie starts to tell some stories about Camp Akiva and the old days. She knows she has an audience that will listen to her.

Jesse climbs into Eli's lap.

"Hey, so . . ." I try to sound natural.

"Spit it out," Ivy says.

"It's just, well, I was supposed to leave soon, but we're actually staying for the rest of the summer."

"For real?" Ivy says.

I nod.

She leans over and hugs me. Then she steals the challah off my plate.

Eli looks at me, shaking his head. "Hey," he says. "I have an idea." He looks at Jesse and then at all of us. "I say we wake up early tomorrow and go fishing."

"Fishing? Yeah!" Jesse shouts.

"But I want to swim," says Ivy.

"Okay," Eli says. "Fish first, then swim. We don't want to scare *all* the fish."

And we knew then that this was an argument that would last the rest of the summer.

79

On a day in late July, Ivy and I go to Duke's stall.

He's waiting for me.

"Good morning, Duke." I give him an apple and then a sugar cube. Ivy brushes his back until his coat shines. Then we lay a blanket onto his back and lift the saddle on. I cinch it until it fits just right.

Outside, Eli and Jesse are already mounted up.

"You guys ready?" Eli asks.

"Yep," Ivy says, handing me a backpack full of food before lifting herself up onto the saddle behind me.

We ride along the first meadow trail—the trail Duke and I went on when I first got here. We pass tall grass, turning brown in the summer heat. We pass the pond.

"Try not to get scared of a turtle when we go by this pond, okay, Duke?" I whisper.

He just goes steadily past. We climb through the cow pasture, going higher, little by little, through woods and canyons until the horse ranch is completely out of sight, the town buildings just dots on the horizon. Ahead of us, we see the old forest and, on the other side, Far Point Meadow. It's my first time coming back to this place since the search for Eli and Star. We wind through the narrow trees, Star far ahead of us now. Duke has his ears all the way back. He doesn't like the narrows. For a moment it feels like the trees press down on us, and even Ivy squeezes tight around my waist. I remember the shadow coyotes and feel my heart beat a little faster.

I breathe in—one, two—and out—one, two.

The sun is bright as we ride into the wide meadow. Trees bloom in tufts of green on every side. I remember the fog from last time. I remember waking up in the Gray.

Breathe in—one, two—and out—one, two.

"C'mon!" Jesse yells, looking back at us. Star is cantering now, moving down through the meadow and the trees to the banks of the water, where the Far Point waterfall crashes into the pool.

I pet Duke's neck. "Soon you can eat all the clover you want, my friend."

Duke whinnies, and we continue to follow Star.

We hike to the banks and stare at the waterfall.

Eli looks at Jesse. "Can you get us back there into the . . . secret spot?"

Jesse smiles and nods.

We follow Jesse along the banks to the far edge of the pool until we're right next to where the water spills down into white foam. Jesse points to a shallow ledge, and then to a rock outcropping just behind where the water is falling.

"No wrong moves," Eli says, looking at all of us. He reaches for his backpack.

"I got it," Ivy says. "Don't worry."

Jesse holds on to a tree limb, leans as close as he can to the small ledge, then lands his foot right on it. Once he's balanced enough, he takes a giant step onto the rock outcropping and steps up, but it's then that he slips. For a second, it looks like he might fall straight into the pool. Eli moves to the edge, but Jesse lands on his behind and starts giggling.

"It's really, really slippery," he says. "Be careful."

So we are, and after a few minutes we've all made it to Jesse's secret spot—a three-walled cave big enough for the four of us to stand in, the fourth wall made of water. We spread out a blanket. Ivy takes out sandwiches and muffins.

We talk about the ride here and make plans for our next ride tomorrow—to the other side of town to a lake with an island right in the middle of it. We eat macaroons that Aunt Ruthie sent along, and Jesse tells us about how he tried surfing in California—and about the time he saw a dolphin in the waves.

I feel the cold floor, made of stone, worn smooth—changed slowly by the trickles of water running down from the walls.

Eli looks at me. "It's a different world in here, Sasha. Don't you think?"

Ivy is listening to Jesse, but she catches what Eli says and looks at me.

"It really is," I say. "A world inside another world. But still all connected. Always changing."

"And that's okay, right?" Ivy says.

I nod, because it's more than okay. It's just right.

EPILOGUE

SOME DAYS LATER . . .

Duke tears along the ground, his body rising into the air and back down with every stride until it feels like we're flying. Behind me, I hear the deep hoofbeats of Warrior, the horse Aunt Ruthie usually rides. My father is trying to keep up. I hold the reins tightly, trying not to pull back too hard. This is the first time I've ever galloped.

We reach a high point over the valley, halfway to Far Point Meadow, and stop to let the horses rest.

"Nice job, Duke," I say, leaning forward and scratching his neck, but he's already combing the ground for clover. My dad leans back in the saddle, takes a long drink of water, and scans the horizon.

"Quite a view," he says. We look from the meadow to the hills beyond. The forest stretches out on either side— giant pines and birch trees under a big cloudy sky. He looks over at some cows lying down beneath a twisted oak. "Aunt Ruthie always says that when the cows sit down it's going to rain. Should we get back?"

I look over at the cows. Lucky is in the center, his horns hovering above his sleepy eyes. Drops of light rain are already falling. I feel the cool drops on my face and look toward the meadow. My heart beats faster. I spend a few moments grounding myself, taking a deep breath, the deepest I can. Then I look at my dad.

"I don't think I want to stop yet. Let's keep going?" He turns Warrior toward the meadow and trots up next to me.

"Lead the way."

AUTHOR'S NOTE

Thank you for reading *The Gray*. Chances are, a lot of people will read this and know what it means when the world gets too big, what it's like to feel anxious and out of control. *The Gray* may be fiction, but it is a story very close to my heart. Much of what Sasha feels, and what he goes through, comes from my own experience.

I was a child of the '80s, when it wasn't common for many people to recognize mental health concerns. So early on in school, whenever I had trouble breathing, or focusing, or even simply talking, I was often told to "get it together," or "control my imagination." They meant well, but I couldn't control any of it. I was nine, and struggling with anxiety disorder.

Thankfully, things have changed, and society is more aware of anxiety as something that many contend with. Yet at the time of writing this book, anxiety for kids is also on the rise. In a recent study, the Centers for Disease Control estimated that over 9 percent of American children suffer from it, and that was before the pandemic forced even more challenges for adults and children alike. The causes are diverse, and disorders like anxiety may manifest differently for everyone.

My hope is that the story of Sasha, an unlikely hero, and his experiences with his friends, family, and the horses in his life, can give insight into a character who is adventurous, imaginative, and thoughtful, despite his many challenges. At the same time, I hope this book helps readers find empathy, and recognize that we all experience fear, stress, and anxiety, and we shouldn't be ashamed of it. Healing and hope can take many forms.

If you feel like you or someone you know is having trouble with anxiety or anything else, there are people out there who care about you. They are waiting to help. Do whatever you can to reach out and take the first step. We may all have a little bit of the Gray inside us, but none of us needs to experience it alone.

ACKNOWLEDGMENTS

Thank you to the village of extraordinary humans (and horses) who helped make this story come alive.

Heartfelt thanks to my incredible literary agent, Rena Rossner, for her tireless work on all the stages of this book, for her honesty, compassion, and guidance, and for always believing in me. Also thanks to the team at DH Literary: Daria Koveshnikov, Talia Harris-Ram, Shira Ben-Choreen Schneck, and Ran Kaiser.

Infinite thanks to wonderful editor extraordinaire, Liz Szabla. Thank you for your brilliance, expertise, and partnership with this very tender story. I consider working with you an absolute gift. Thanks to the whole amazing team at Feiwel & Friends: Rich Deas (Senior Creative Director), Arik Hardin (Assistant Managing Editor), Kim Waymer (Senior Production Manager), Kelsey Marrujo (Assistant Director, Publicity), and Mary Van Akin (Director, School & Library Marketing). Also to intern Sage Kiernan-Sherrow for all the work making this book come to life, and of course a huge thanks to Jean Feiwel for always making me feel at home at F&F.

Huge thanks to Celia Krampien for her gorgeous vision for the cover illustration. Thank you for perfectly capturing the spirit of Sasha and the heart of the story and its many settings.

Thank you to the teachers, librarians, and educators who put books in the hands of kids who need them, always looking out for the kids who might be lost, quiet, or in need. Thank you to the healthcare professionals who worked with me on this story, offered expert advice and counseling, and who work tirelessly with kids and families every day.

Heartfelt thanks to all my friends, family, and community, who walk with me through this writing journey. I could not do any of it without you. Immense thanks to my writing people for wrestling with my silliest and most serious ideas. Special thanks to those of you who read various versions of this book and helped to shape it: Josh Levy (for calls at all hours), Ally Malinenko, Rajani LaRocca, Jessica Redman, the JPST, Nick and Denie Bailey, and so many others.

Special thanks to my Krav Maga Instructors: Yury and Veronica, and to all my training partners at Impact Krav Maga for all the years of training, mentorship, and experiences.

Thanks to all the landscapes in my life that are threaded in my heart and find their way into this book: New York City where I grew up and the small towns upstate where I lived, and to the horses I loved: Gus, Flash, and Shawnee. So glad to see you riding again through these pages.

And of course, I'm so grateful for my family: my mother and father, who moved us from the city to the country because they wanted to save our lives. Thank you to my whole family, who many of the characters in this book are based on: Aunt Cookie, Sam and Mae Rosensweig, Steve Rosensweig, Edith, Paul, and Andrew Vegoda, Stacey Wink, Steve Kramer, and Maggie Flack.

Most of all, thank you to my beautiful and fearless wife, Ella, and my kids, Sasha, Samaria, and Caylao, for their unconditional love and support.

Lastly, to all the readers out there who may be like some of the kids in this book, thank you for your courage, your inspiration, and your willingness to change the world.

THANK YOU FOR READING THIS FEIWEL AND FRIENDS BOOK.
THE FRIENDS WHO MADE

THE GRAY

POSSIBLE ARE:

Jean Feiwel, *Publisher*

Liz Szabla, *VP, Associate Publisher*

Rich Deas, *Senior Creative Director*

Holly West, *Senior Editor*

Anna Roberto, *Senior Editor*

Kat Brzozowski, *Senior Editor*

Dawn Ryan, *Executive Managing Editor*

Kim Waymer, *Senior Production Manager*

Emily Settle, *Editor*

Rachel Diebel, *Editor*

Foyinsi Adegbonmire, *Associate Editor*

Brittany Groves, *Assistant Editor*

Arik Hardin, *Assistant Managing Editor*

FOLLOW US ON FACEBOOK OR VISIT US ONLINE AT
MACKIDS.COM. OUR BOOKS ARE FRIENDS FOR LIFE.